T0312293

# The Spicy Bedtime Companion

# *The Spicy*
# Bedtime Companion

EROTIC STORIES AND MORE

JOAN ELIZABETH LLOYD

HEAT | NEW YORK

THE BERKLEY PUBLISHING GROUP
Published by the Penguin Group
Penguin Group (USA) Inc.
375 Hudson Street, New York, New York 10014, USA
Penguin Group (Canada), 90 Eglinton Avenue East, Suite 700, Toronto, Ontario M4P 2Y3, Canada
(a division of Pearson Penguin Canada Inc.)
Penguin Books Ltd., 80 Strand, London WC2R 0RL, England
Penguin Group Ireland, 25 St. Stephen's Green, Dublin 2, Ireland (a division of Penguin Books Ltd.)
Penguin Group (Australia), 250 Camberwell Road, Camberwell, Victoria 3124, Australia
(a division of Pearson Australia Group Pty. Ltd.)
Penguin Books India Pvt. Ltd., 11 Community Centre, Panchsheel Park, New Delhi—110 017, India
Penguin Group (NZ), 67 Apollo Drive, Rosedale, North Shore 0632, New Zealand
(a division of Pearson New Zealand Ltd.)
Penguin Books (South Africa) (Pty.) Ltd., 24 Sturdee Avenue, Rosebank, Johannesburg 2196,
South Africa

Penguin Books Ltd., Registered Offices: 80 Strand, London WC2R 0RL, England

This book is an original publication of The Berkley Publishing Group.

This is a work of fiction. Names, characters, places, and incidents either are the product of the author's imagination or are used fictitiously, and any resemblance to actual persons, living or dead, business establishments, events, or locales is entirely coincidental. The publisher does not have any control over and does not assume any responsibility for author or third-party websites or their content.

PRINTING HISTORY
Heat trade paperback edition / September 2009

Library of Congress Cataloging-in-Publication Data

Lloyd, Joan Elizabeth.
    The spicy bedtime companion / Joan Elizabeth Lloyd.—Heat trade pbk. ed.
        p.   cm.
    ISBN 978-0-425-22983-5 (trade pbk.)
    I. Title.
    PS3562.L72S6   2009
    813'.54—dc22

                                                                        2009013296

147204767

# Contents

The Spicy Bedtime Companion

# The Game

⟨ornament⟩

IT'S CALLED *HEDONISM*. I DON'T KNOW WHETHER YOU could call it a game but in the underground gaming world where it was created and is secretly distributed, it's referred to as a game. Game? There are no lands to explore, monsters to fight or jewels to be found. Maidens to win? You bet.

Here's how it works: It's sort of a role-playing game, played both on your own computer and through the Internet connection, sort of like *Guild Wars* or *World of Warcraft*. But different. Very different.

Since *Hedonism* is based on virtual reality you wear a sort of net bodysuit with lots of little gizmos that let the program know what your arms and legs are doing. It even has a cowl with a face covering so all your expressions can be conveyed to the screen. Play begins when you sit at your computer and select a new persona, or reuse one you've used before.

Hmm. Let me get out of generalizations and tell you about my most recent encounter. Yeah, I guess *encounter* is the best way to write this. Although I'm not a professional writer, I've read lots of stories—I particularly like sci-fi—so I'll write this as best as I can. Please forgive my inability to fully describe everything.

Last evening I hurried home from work, grabbing a Big Mac and fries on the way, and dumped my coat and briefcase on the bed in my little studio apartment. Then I stripped to my shorts. I like it better that way, although the first few times I played I kept my jeans and shirt on. I would get naked but I need the shorts—you'll see why later. I slipped the net stocking over my mostly bare skin.

I logged on to the site and selected the identity I like best. In this one I'm a knight in full armor—lance, sword, shield and all. On the screen my hair is blond as it is in real life, but I have a cute little goatee. I'm better-looking on the screen too, with a handsome face and a well-developed body, one I modeled on Patrick Swayze in *Dirty Dancing*. I had a girlfriend several months ago who loved that film and, although it's a real chick flick, one evening I watched it with her. She loved the guy and was so turned on by the end of the film that we rolled around on my bed for over an hour. I think Patrick has a great, sexy body and, because of her reaction, his moves are the ones I want for my knight.

I clicked on "Start Game." That's the last thing I had to do with my keyboard or mouse so I stood up and watched the screen.

I'm on a forest path and my horse is standing off to one side chomping on grass. I can almost smell the greenery, and birds are chirping. Although I know the scenario by heart my pulse still speeds up as I wait for her to appear. And she does.

She's the most beautiful woman I can imagine and she fits my desires to a tee. Of course she could be nothing else since I created her two months ago and have been refining her ever since. Now she's the perfect height, coming just to my cheek, with long, heavy black hair that hangs down her back, deep blue eyes and a face that all my friends would stare at. She's dressed in a see-through gown that shows off her body, and she's the hottest thing I've ever seen. Great tits with big, smoky nipples, long legs, a thatch of black hair that always makes my fingers itch.

"Good evening, Sir Knight," she says, her voice soft and breathy. She sounds so natural that it's hard for me to remember that her voice is coming from my computer speakers. No, I don't want to think about that.

"Good evening." As I speak, my character on the screen forms the words with his lifelike mouth.

"I've been waiting for you." She walks toward me and kisses me on my lips. I can feel her kiss. I know that's spooky, but I can. It's as if I've become the knight on the screen. I lift my arms and hold her close. Of course it's the sensors that make it all work but . . .

"Ooh," she says, "your armor is so cold that it freezes my breasts."

I look down and, indeed, I can see through her gown that her nipples are fully erect. "Sorry," I say and, with a nod of my head, the armor is gone. I can feel its weight lifted from my body. How odd. Then I touch her shoulders and I can actually feel her skin. I slide my hands down her arms to warm her and she looks at me and smiles.

Watching her I'm getting a hard-on and, as my cock grows, the cock on the knight grows too. "Shall we go somewhere private?" she says.

She takes my hand and leads me to a little clearing several paces off the roadway. Somehow I know that no one else in the game knows about this spot and we'll be totally alone. There's a blanket spread on the grass and she gracefully settles on it. The gown does little to cover her beautiful body, and my cock grows more insistent. I nod again and the rest of my clothing melts away until I'm standing before her looking fabulous, with my oversized dick sticking straight out from my groin. She knows just what to do.

She gets up on her knees and cups my balls. I can feel her fingers lightly massaging my sac and I watch her lick her lips. Fluid oozes from my dick both on the screen and in reality, and it twitches. "Mmm," she purrs, "you're really eager for me."

Eager? I'm so hot I could burst, but I don't. Yet.

Then her mouth is on me and I can feel the heat of her tongue as she licks the length of me, grazing my stalk with her teeth. She's perfect at giving head. As she pulls back she makes a little vacuum so my cock resists withdrawing. Then she sucks harder and again my dick is drawn inside.

The small part of my mind that can still function tells my hands to squeeze her tits, so I bend slightly and, her mouth still sucking, I take one large boob in each hand and pinch her nipples. Her mouth jerks with the joy of it and she makes these sexy little sounds of pleasure.

I want to fuck her, and maybe one day I will, but for now I'm too hot to do anything but let her suck me off. I feel come boil in my belly and erupt, soaking the inside of my shorts. Now you understand why I play with them on.

She purrs and I can feel the vibration on my now-softening dick. "That's wonderful," she says softly, pulling away from my now-satisfied body. "Come again soon."

The screen slowly dissolves into the game's logo. *Hedonism*. I drop onto the bed, satiated, still wearing the sensor net. Maybe I'll play again later.

Of course I will. Often.

# Vivid Dreaming

I GUESS IT'S ONE OF THE MEDICATIONS I'M TAKING. It doesn't matter why I'm taking stuff; suffice it to say I'm feeling great. Anyway, something is causing me to have amazingly vivid dreams. Not nightmares, just incredibly detailed, realistic dreams. I mean dreams that feel so real that it's difficult to realize that I was asleep or that I'm awake afterward. Most are truly benign, like I'm taking the kids to school, or I'm having dinner at Rick's parents' house. Like that. Not sexy, just . . . there. However, one night recently things changed.

I went to bed really horny. Unfortunately Rick had had a really long day at work so when he drifted off to sleep quickly I didn't have the heart to wake him. Since it was deep winter and I was a little chilly I snuggled against Rick and enjoyed the feel of his warm, firm, sexy body against me. Sexy body? It was the middle of the night and he was snoring away yet I was thinking sexy. What the heck could I do? So I turned on my side and fell asleep.

Suddenly I knew I was dreaming. The room was the one I grew up in at my folks' house and I was in my narrow single bed. There was a little light coming in from under my door so I could see my old dresser, desk and the braided rug my grandmother had made. I felt like a teenager, not like a thirty-five-year-old housewife. Okay, you must be dreaming, I told myself.

I looked over and Rick was in the tiny bed with me, his back against my chest. But it wasn't my Rick. It was the Rick I'd met almost eighteen years ago, in his late teens with long, soft, shiny hair and a hard, athletic body. Weird, no? And very confusing. I smiled to myself. What we wouldn't have given back then for a bed and time to enjoy it.

Okay, so in my dream Rick rolled over. I could hear his light snoring but I also saw the tent that had formed over his cock. I wanted him to be aroused. You can bet on that.

I was hungry for him, so I decided to take matters into my own hands. Literally. I slipped my hands beneath the covers. In my dream it was beneath the lacy pink quilt of back then.

I slid my hands over Rick's chest, feeling the tight abs he'd had then. God, I've always loved his body, despite the slight paunch he has now. Let me tell you that Rick has very sensitive nipples. I found this out recently, quite by accident. We were making love and I brushed my fingernails over his flat, male nipples and felt him flinch. I thought I'd hurt him, and I apologized. His face flushed and he informed me that, rather than injuring him, I'd heightened his arousal. I guess he didn't think it was manly to have nipples that tightened when he was excited, but I loved it. Now he had a magic button as I did.

I wanted to see whether this Rick would also respond so I flicked my fingernail over his tit and felt it get hard. Oh yeah, I thought. Things don't change, at least in my dreams. I pushed the covers back and leaned over him, lapping at his tight little nub. He squirmed but the bed was so narrow that he couldn't back away. He quickly settled down and continued his light snoring.

I've never been an aggressive lover. It's sort of embarrassing for me to make the moves, but this is a different situation. It's fun, I thought. I can play and eventually, when I wake up, Rick won't be the wiser.

I licked at his chest and neck and watched his cock react. I quickly learned that little nips on his neck got him harder, while biting his shoulder cooled him somewhat. My own little truth machine.

It was still very chilly in the room so I ducked beneath the covers and found his navel. I pushed my tongue in and again he squirmed. Good? Bad? When he tried to wiggle away I decided to go for the gold. I wrapped my fingers around his hard cock and squeezed. I ran my finger over the head and felt his wetness. Yeah, he was hot, all right.

I love the taste of my husband, then and now, so I slowly licked the precome from his beautiful penis, while stroking his shaft with my fist. Gradually I took him in my mouth, slowly enveloping his cock, licking the tip as more and more fluid leaked out.

My head bobbing over his cock, I fucked him with my mouth. He got as hard as I've ever felt. I wriggled around until I could reach my pussy, but at that moment Rick said, "Oh, no, you don't."

With a low growl, he pushed me onto my back and mounted me. He wasted no time on any more preliminaries, but plunged into me, big and hard and so wonderful. I needed him so much and his cock filled me completely. His fingers didn't leave my clit and I came. I've never done that before.

He held still for just a moment, then said, his voice hoarse, "Shit, baby, I can really feel your climax." I grabbed his head and pulled his mouth to mine as he thrust, his powerful muscles ramming his cock into me over and over.

He stifled a bellow as he came, his dick deep inside me, pouring his gism into my body.

Panting, he rolled off of me and pulled me close against his side. Please, I thought, I don't want to wake up yet.

"God, that was amazing," I purred.

"It was that," Rick rumbled.

I opened my eyes and looked at him. I was startled to see that it was my Rick, in his thirties, hairline beginning to recede, his slight paunch, with a totally bemused look on his face. I glanced around. It was my bedroom in the house Rick and I had bought eight years before.

Was I awake? Now I was totally confused. There was no denying that orgasm. I was leaking between my legs, making a wet spot in the bed.

"I loved that," Rick said, his speech becoming slurred with impending sleep. "When you grabbed me from a sound sleep it took only moments for me to get hard. Do that more often, will you?" He yawned and in moments I could hear his regular breathing become deeper and more regular.

What had happened? Where had the dream ended and reality begun? I tried to figure it out, then decided that it didn't matter. Rick and I had just had some of the hottest sex we'd had since we were first married. I just knew that the next time I woke up in the middle of the night I would grab him and try for a replay of tonight. Wow! How fabulous!

# The Golden Spa

THE BRIDESMAIDS' DRESSES WERE A GORGEOUS SHADE OF burgundy, and when the four of us tried the dresses on, I looked really good. Actually so did the others. My dress fit like it was made for me so I took it home from the bridal shop and impatiently waited the two weeks until the Sunday wedding.

With three kids and a part-time job, I don't have a lot of time for myself. My folks decided to help Jeremy and me out so they took all three boys on Friday night so we could enjoy an evening and get to the wedding on time the following day. I arranged my work schedule so that I had Friday afternoon off. My time! Three whole hours before Jeremy got home from work.

I'd driven past the Golden Spa several times but I never considered going in until that week. Hell, I reasoned, I had an afternoon to myself and, after all, didn't I deserve a little "me" stuff every hundred years?

So just after lunch I walked in. Immediately I loved the smell of the beauty products, the sound of the soft, relaxing music, and I felt myself unwinding. I'm worth it, I thought. I was greeted by a tiny Asian woman and, with only a little coaxing, I signed up for a massage and a manicure and pedicure.

I'd never had a massage and at this place it wasn't really a nude thing. They had a special chair and I sat and put my face against the padded sides of this little opening. "Just relax," the woman said as she began my half hour with my hands. It was sensual without being sexual, just amazingly relaxing. Hands, arms, shoulders, any more relaxed and I'd be a puddle. As she worked on my back, occasionally her hands moved to my sides and the ends of her fingers brushed the sides of my breasts. It was all totally innocent, but it added a hint of spice to my body.

When she was done I moved to the pedicure chair and spent another half hour having my legs and feet scrubbed and massaged. Jeremy loves my feet and he's given me several foot massages over the years. I guess I tend to associate having my toes rubbed with eroticism so, despite the totally clinical attitude of the woman doing my pedicure, the entire experience was revving my engine. I had picked a color that seemed closest to the color of my dress from the dozens of bottles on the wall and eventually she polished each toenail.

Next came the manicure. Suddenly I heard myself saying, "What would it take to give me long, sexy nails?" I'd always had short, utilitarian nails that broke often and usually looked pretty lousy. For this wedding, and for Jeremy, I wanted really

sexy ones in dark burgundy. Hooker nails, I thought. He'd occasionally commented on the long nails of someone in a movie
so I thought he'd like that.

"I would need about an hour," the attractive woman said,
and she quoted a price.

"What the hell. Let's do it."

For all of sixty minutes she applied long, curved plastic
shapes, cut, filed and glued, then painted on several layers of
polish. I sat with lights and fans blowing on my fingers and toes
and finally paid the bill.

I got into my car and couldn't keep my eyes off my fingers.
I tapped the nails on the steering wheel in the galloping-horses
rhythm I'd heard my friends do. As I headed home I kept staring at my hands. I loved those sexy nails.

As I pulled into our driveway, I glanced at my watch. Jeremy
would be home in just a few minutes so I didn't have much
time.

I went upstairs to check how the color of my nails matched
the color of the dress. In my right mind I don't think I could
have done what I did next, but I wasn't in my right mind. Or
maybe I was—oh, so right.

I found the jacket that went over the dress and discovered
that I'd been accurate. The color was perfect. I stood, thought
about my massage and pedicure and the sexy way they made
me feel. So I stripped off my clothes and put on a pair of tiny
bikini panties and slipped into the jacket. Nothing more, just
the panties and the jacket. I've got pretty good cleavage, even
without a bra, and with only one button on the jacket, it
showed to its best advantage. I looked down and had to admit

to myself that I looked hot. Then I slipped on a pair of thigh-high stockings and buckled on the strappy sandals I was going to wear the following day.

I resisted the temptation to look in the mirror. I was afraid I'd chicken out. But I was pretty sure how Jeremy would react, and I wanted him. It was just that simple.

I heard the door from the garage close. "Missy, I'm home," Jeremy called.

"I'll be down in a second."

I took a deep breath, straightened my spine, sucked in my stomach and descended the stairs.

Jeremy had his back to me so I stopped halfway down. "How was your day?" I asked, my voice low and husky.

"Fine," he said, then turned. The expression on his face was worth any embarrassment I might have felt. "Wow. Let me have a good look at you."

I posed on the steps for a moment as his eyes raked my body, then did a slinky walk most of the way down. I thought I might be a little over the top but obviously Jeremy didn't think so. The expression on his face was so hungry I thought that, given half a chance, he'd devour me whole.

"You look amazing," he said, his breathing already a little fast as he approached the foot of the stairs and stood slightly below me. His gaze slid over me, paying special attention to my new nails. "I was going to ask how your day was, but obviously I don't have to."

"It was wonderful and I thought I'd enjoy the end of it too."

"You bet." He took one of my hands and licked each nail. "These are sexy as hell." Then I bent down a little so Jeremy could take me in his arms and kiss me. He's a great kisser, his lips soft and warm on mine, changing the position on his mouth frequently to increase the connection. "God, baby," he said against my lips. "You look so hot."

I tangled my fingers in his hair and deepened the kiss. Then his mouth wandered down my neck and onto my breastbone. I allowed my head to fall back as he covered my skin with tiny kisses and love bites.

Then he unfastened the one button that held the front of my jacket closed and moved a step down so his mouth was level with my breasts. His hands slithered up beneath the jacket and braced my body against the onslaught of his lips. He knows that I love to have my breasts kissed and suckled so he took a long time making love to my flesh. God, it felt so good. My knees went weak, my pussy twitched and my juices flowed, soaking the crotch of my tiny panties.

He licked one nipple, then blew on it, the cool air making the bud tighten still more until it was almost painful. Then he repeated his actions with the other. He slid his fingers to my sides and teased the sides of my breasts, then cupped them, holding them against his mouth.

I was so aroused I thought I couldn't get any higher, but when he pulled down my panties and his thumbs found my slit, I almost screamed. He guided me down until I was sitting on the thickly carpeted steps; then he put my legs over his shoulders. "You're so wet," he purred with a leer. "I'll bet I can make you come with just my mouth. Let's give it a try."

Usually I needed to be filled with Jeremy's big cock to climax but I was so high I thought he might be right. His tongue flicked over my erect clit while his thumbs parted my inner lips. Then he licked the length of me. I lay back on the steps and closed my eyes, concentrating on the magic his mouth was working on my pussy.

When he sucked on my clit and rubbed my inner lips with his fingers I screamed and climaxed. He kept up the stimulation, and it was as if I couldn't finish. The spasms kept rocketing through my body until I thought I'd expire from the pleasure.

Finally, when my body calmed just a bit, Jeremy backed away slightly, unzipped his jeans and, still fully clothed, pounded his erection into me.

I grabbed the back of his head, then scratched his neck with my new, long nails. "Shit," he hissed, pulling his shirt off over his head without pulling out. My nails raked his back, enough to leave marks but not draw blood. As my hands cupped his ass cheeks and my nails made little dents in his skin, he cried out and, with an arch of his back and a last thrust of his hips, he followed me over the edge with a husky roar of satisfaction.

"Let me see those nails," he said later. I held out one hand. "God, those are so sexy. Would it be too difficult to keep them that way? They make me hot."

The Golden Spa had a new customer.

# The South of France

THIS ALL BEGAN WITH TWO TOTALLY UNRELATED EVENTS two weeks ago. I got an e-mail from a good friend of mine and I ran out of antacids.

Okay, first the antacids. I make a very, very good living trading commodities for a large firm. It's a stressful job, and I do mean stressful. I've got a seven-figure bank account all right and I'm only thirty-one, but sometimes I feel fifty-one and slowly but surely the stress is killing me. I know I'm stressed but do nothing about it. I merely pop antacids like candy and keep on. One evening I ran out. None. Anywhere. I was so sick most of the night that first thing the following morning I drove to the doctor. He examined me and gave me a stern talking-to. He told me in no uncertain terms that I was shortening my life. It definitely got me thinking.

Then came the e-mail. The following day it was in my in-box, a note from an old friend named Cassie. She and three other women I knew had been all ready to take a trip to the south of France, until Meg broke her leg. Now they had plane reservations, hotel rooms booked and a rental car with only three of them going. Would I consider getting away for a week?

I could picture all the women's faces. We had been quite a group in college, great friends and sorority sisters. Something was speaking to me. Get away, it was saying. Just take off. I'll think about it, I told myself as I reread Cassie's note. I immediately called Meg, told her how badly I felt about her accident and offered to help with anything she needed. She told me she was all set. "Did Cassie tell you about the trip?" she asked. "You have to go in my place. The south of France. It's all planned and you'll have a ball. Pâté, sausages, great bread and all the lovely French wine." We chatted for a few more minutes; then I hung up. Do it! a voice in my head was saying.

I phoned Cassie and we chatted like no time had passed since we last shared secrets. Do it! So I said yes. On a whim. Just like that. I realized how fabulous it felt to do something just because it felt good. And it would be great for my psyche.

The plane was leaving in three days, so I closed out all my positions in the market, looked up the weather on the Internet and put a bunch of stuff in a suitcase. Of course I arranged for a phone that would keep me informed about the markets, had Web access that worked all over Europe. I told my boss I was taking off and she was delighted. "You need a rest. Have a blast. Screw a hot guy or two while you're away."

"Fat chance," I said, laughing.

"Don't close any doors; that's all I'm saying," she said.

Whatever.

We arrived in Marseilles, picked up our rental car and headed east along the coast. Cassie, Paula, Lily and I laughed and I felt better and better. I did keep my phone handy and checked in with the markets every evening. Actually it was frustrating, since there was a six-hour time difference, but I managed.

We were sitting in a sidewalk café having lunch when a hunk, and I do mean hunk, parked his motorcycle across the little square and climbed off. He was wearing a tight tee shirt and pair of shorts that left little to the imagination. He pulled off his helmet and I saw a head of thick blond, curly hair and deep blue eyes.

He seemed to stare right at me. He put one foot up on the fender of the bike and just stood, gazing at me. I'm not so much to look at, I guess, but his frank appraisal made me feel sexy and gorgeous. Reality didn't matter.

I found myself gazing right back at him until, minutes later, he crooked his finger at me, then pointed to the rear seat on the vehicle. His invitation was both unbelievable and irresistible. Could I? I could hear my boss's voice. *"Screw a hot guy or two while you're away."*

Without another word I stood up, crossed the grassy area and got onto the back of the bike. He handed me a helmet, put his on, climbed on in front of me and off we went. Not a word, not a touch, nothing. It was wonderful. The air rushing by, the feeling of the engine roaring—I hadn't felt so free, and I will admit sexy, in a long, long time.

I slid my arms around his body and felt the washboard abs beneath his tee shirt. I leaned against his back and smelled the combination of his aftershave and his own personal scent and reveled in the sensations.

I paid no attention to my surroundings until he stopped the bike on a narrow path, deep in the countryside. The tiny byway was lined with trees and there was no one around.

He turned in his seat until he was straddling the bike backward. He pulled off his helmet and I removed mine. I knew what was going to happen and I wanted it as badly as I'd wanted anything in a long time. My nipples were hard and tight and my panties were soaked.

He grabbed the sides of my top and pulled it off over my head, then deftly removed my bra. His fingers were incredibly talented, alternately pulling my nipples and swirling over my flesh. I moaned with the pleasure of it all.

Then his mouth found one nipple and sucked, hard. I was in heaven as shafts of pleasure shot from my breasts to my pussy. I was so hot I thought I'd explode, but he wasn't in any hurry. He suckled, tweaked, played, teased until I was going crazy.

His hands moved to my knees and slid up my thighs, his thumbs doing devilish things to the soft skin at the inside. I wanted his hands on my clit but when I reached for him he pushed my hands away. I leaned back against the bike's small backrest and resigned myself to doing it all at his speed. I let go of everything.

Then his fingers found my panties and pulled the crotch aside. His thumb found my clit as he slid two fingers deep inside me.

I shot to the moon, screaming in my climax.

He got off the bike and removed his clothing, then pulled me off and easily undressed me. Then he sat back on the bike and positioned me in front of him, facing him. Lifting me, he impaled me on his thick, hard shaft. Then he started the bike and revved the engine. I came again and again as he thrust.

"Earth to Martha," Cassie's voice said. "Hello?"

I was still sitting at the café with my three friends, and the cute guy on the motorcycle was gone. However, my panties were soaked and I was breathing hard. Not wanting my friends to tease me, I controlled my respirations. "You've really got to relax more, babe," she continued. "You drift off into Wall Street land much too often."

If she only knew. I saw my phone on the table and closed it, put it into my purse and vowed to live. Really live. Maybe I'll buy a motorcycle.

# Through the Walls

IT WAS TUESDAY EVENING AND I WAS ON A BUSINESS TRIP to a midwestern city. I was exhausted from daylong negotiations so, after a quick dinner at a fast-food joint, I checked into my motel, stripped off my clothes, dropped onto the predictable flowered, satin quilt and flipped on the TV. I tuned to an all-news channel, called my wife, spoke to her only briefly, then lapsed into unconsciousness.

I slept for a few hours, then was awakened by the couple next door. My company has a limited number of reimbursable motels and they tend to be cheapies, so the walls are usually pretty thin. This place was no exception. I could hear what was going on as if the two people were in the same room.

"Oh, baby," a female voice said through the wall, "I love it when you do that."

"I love touching you and watching you get hot," the male voice replied.

I quickly muted the TV, wondering whether they'd notice the sudden silence, but I guess they were too far gone to pay any attention. She squealed, "Push your fingers in. Harder." A few moments of heavy breathing; then she yelled, "Pull my panties off! I want you now!"

"No fucking just yet," he said and she giggled. A moment's silence; then he gasped. "You shaved your snatch. Holy shit, I can see everything."

"I thought you'd like it."

"Shit, baby, I do. Wow. Okay, now lift your hips so I can suck on your beautiful, naked pussy." I could hear him moan. "That's sooooo sexy."

During the moments of silence that ensued I pictured his face between her legs, tongue licking and probing on her hairless cunt. I could picture her naked flesh, just like the porno films I sometimes watch when I'm away. I closed my eyes and let the pictures fill my mind. I was probably hallucinating, but I could swear I heard slurping sounds and lots of heavy breathing.

By now my cock was getting really hard and, since I was lying naked on the bedspread, I looked down and watched my pecker twitch. In my mind I could almost feel it sinking into the woman's naked pussy.

"Shit, baby," she said, "you're making me crazy."

He laughed, then said, "I know." More slurping.

I couldn't keep my hand still. It was as though my fingers reached down of their own volition and grasped my dick. I closed my eyes again and listened. I felt like the worst kind of voyeur, and I loved it.

"Come here," she said, "so I can taste myself on your lips."

Damn, damn, I was getting so hot I could almost shoot my load right then, but I wanted to wait just a little longer. In the silence he must have moved up, and they kissed. "I love it when you taste of me, but it's my turn now."

Oh shit, I thought, I'm going to have to listen to her suck him off and I've got no way to relieve myself except by using my hand. As I stroked I tried to picture making love to my lovely wife but I was too far gone, my mind filled with the image of the two lovers in the next room.

"Shit, baby," he groaned. "You've got the best mouth. Suck it more, harder."

"Oh baby," I whispered, "suck me too." My hand rubbed my cock from base to tip and I could imagine her mouth on the head.

"More, more." Then he said, "Shit, baby, you'd better stop or I'll shoot in your mouth."

"Would that be so bad?"

"I want your cunt. Now!"

She purred loudly. "I wouldn't want to keep you waiting, would I? If you want me, come here."

Bedsprings squeaked as they rearranged themselves; then the inevitable rhythmic groan of the bed and the moaning noises began. Over and over he must have thrust into her, and my hand beat my dick in the same rhythm. I'm a noisy lover so I jammed my other fist into my mouth as I came, filling my fist with my gism. Then the guy next door came as well, but with a bellow. I laughed quietly as I relaxed my arms. I could have yelled my lungs out and never been heard over his shout, which was quickly followed by her high-pitched scream.

I calmed, as I guess they did as well. I used the bathroom to clean myself up, then glanced at the clock. It was only ten twenty, so I flipped my cell phone open and called my wife. "You weren't asleep, were you, babe?" I asked when she picked up.

"Nope. I was watching the news, getting ready to climb into bed. You sounded really beat before. Did you get a nap?"

Boy, that and more, I thought. "I did, and I dreamed about you. I love you and I can't tell you how much I miss you."

She sighed, long and low. "I miss you too, darling."

"Only two more days and I'll be home. I can't wait to get you in bed."

My wife's familiar deep chuckle filled the receiver. "Had a wet dream, did you?"

"You can't imagine. I'll tell you all about it when I get home. And I do mean all about it."

"Now you've got me curious." She's got the sexiest laugh.

"You'll have to wait, but be ready for some great stuff," I said, using our slang for good fucking. "I love you and I miss you."

"I love you too, baby. Now you've got me so keyed up I won't be able to sleep."

"They say masturbation is a great soporific. You should try it sometime."

I heard her gasp as I flipped the phone closed.

## In Case You Were Wondering

- The blue whale holds the record for the largest penis of any living animal at about ten feet long and one foot in diameter. The sperm whale is only a bit smaller, at about nine feet at greatest length. Oh, and the name "sperm whale" comes from the fact that whalers found a slimy, oily substance in its head and thought it was, indeed, sperm.

- The walrus has the largest penis bone of any land animal, measuring at its best more than two feet long.

- The rhino can ejaculate ten times in a half-hour "love-making session."

- Most turkeys and giraffes are bisexual.

- Certain male monkeys greet one another by showing off their penises.

- Some male moths can smell a virgin moth from 1.8 miles away.

- Female gorillas are fertile, and thus available, for only six days in every four-year cycle, so that, on average, most males only get any once a year.

- A chimpanzee mating lasts about three seconds. How's that for a quickie?

- One bull can ejaculate enough semen to fertilize three hundred cows.

- A mouse's sperm is actually longer than that of an elephant.

- Measuring seventeen inches in length, a species of lake duck has the longest penis of any bird.

- A rattlesnake mating can last as long as twenty-two hours.

- Male bats have the highest rate of homosexuality of any mammal.

# Magic Mirror

$\mathcal{I}$ HAVE A MAGIC MIRROR. OKAY, I KNOW YOU'RE THINKING that there are lots of magic mirrors out there in some castle or other, but my magic mirror is different. Well, I don't know that it's different because if there are others of this kind out there, I might not have heard of them. It's all pretty private. Why? My mirror pleasures me, physically.

How to explain this . . . ?

The mirror is a full-length, freestanding oval glass with a gold frame and a few precious stones around the edges. I don't know when it appeared in my room, but it wasn't too long ago.

Before the mirror arrived, most evenings I would go up to my room, feeling very, well, horny. I haven't got a prince yet, handsome or otherwise, and I can't risk doing it with someone in the household, so sexual gratification has to be a personal thing, if at all. Anyway, when I'm feeling needy, I go up to my room, let my maid undress me and help me into my nightgown. Then she leaves. Sometimes I touch myself but that seems so naughty, so most of the time I just go to bed hungry.

Since the mirror arrived, each evening I hurry to my room and make quick work about changing into night clothing. I think my maid suspects what goes on, or at least she thinks I get my rocks off somehow. She couldn't imagine what really happens. No one could.

Anyway, now I don't need any help from my own hands. I merely stand before my magic mirror and watch. My reflection is naked, as if I can see right through my garment. Then the hands appear. Just hands. Disembodied hands. Oh, rest assured it's not icky. Nooooo, not at all.

How did it start?

THE MIRROR HAD BEEN IN MY ROOM ONLY A FEW DAYS. IT stood in the corner as if waiting for me. One evening shortly after its arrival, as I sat on the edge of my bed, brushing my long hair and preparing to retire, I turned and gazed into it. Disembodied hands slowly materialized and stroked down my sides from ribs to flanks. I jumped to my feet and whirled to see who was behind me. There was no one there, but I could still feel the hands on my skin as if they were real. Warm, soft, smooth skin against mine.

They felt so good that, rather than being frightened and calling for help, or at least jumping into my bed and pulling the covers over my head, I turned back to stare into the mirror and

I let the hands touch me. Eventually, after five minutes or so, they faded away, leaving me somehow satisfied.

I was really curious to see whether the scene might be repeated so, the following evening, I dashed up the stairs—as quickly as a princess is allowed to dash, of course—and into my room. As always my maid got me ready for bed and left. I stood before the mirror and soon the hands appeared again against my naked skin. They felt so real that I glanced down and reassured myself that I was still dressed in white cotton. No hands in reality, just in the mirror.

This time they stroked my sides, and then the fingers wandered leisurely to cup my breasts. I actually felt them lift my flesh, weighing, squeezing. God, it felt good.

Now, understand that I'm a virgin and I've never felt the touch of a real man. However, I'm not an idiot and I know, or at least I've imagined, how good the touch of a man will be. *Eventually.* Now *eventually* was here.

Then the hands again disappeared.

For the next several nights I arrived in my room, got changed and stood before my reflection. The hands got bolder each evening. One night they stroked the skin on my breasts, swirling toward my now-erect nipples; the next they brushed the tips with their palms. The following night they pinched my erect buds, and my knees became so weak with the pleasure of it that I almost collapsed.

I wanted to let the pleasure carry me away, so the following evening I pulled a chair in front of the mirror and sat while the hands stroked and caressed me. I closed my eyes and let my head fall back, but when I stopped gazing into the mirror the hands disappeared. Okay, I couldn't close my eyes so from then on I gazed fixedly at my reflection.

Finally the hands got so skilled at playing with my breasts that I actually climaxed just from that. The feeling was so strange that I didn't recognize it at first for what it was. My pussy became incredibly wet, my clitoris twitched and suddenly small spasms took over my body. It was amazing. Wonderful and, I feared, addicting.

I found a few books in the secret part of my father's library—I wonder whether my mother knows that he has books about that sort of thing—and read about orgasms. Ahh, the power of education.

For the better part of a week—and it was the better part, I assure you—the hands used my breasts to drive me to climax. Then one fateful evening the hands stopped, leaving me really high. At first I worried that they'd left me, but they quickly slid down my sides to my belly. They rubbed and caressed, finally combing through my pubic hair. I parted my thighs.

I didn't really do it of my own volition; it just happened. Okay, okay, I'll fess up. I did part them myself, hoping the hands would continue what they'd begun. And they did. Slowly one finger slipped into the crevice and found my clit, already hard and swollen. One touch on it and I came. I swallowed my screams of pleasure.

Once I'd come, the hands disappeared.

Then began a week of rubbing and stroking, efficiently bringing me to orgasm every night. That brings me to today.

\* \* \*

I FINISHED DINNER AND RUSHED TO MY ROOM. AS ALWAYS, the maid hustled out and I quickly moved the chair so I could gaze into the mirror. So now here I sit. I am so hungry that I think the hands could bring me off without any sensation at all, just by watching them.

They appear from behind the chair and begin to play with my breasts. I concentrate on the fingers as they tease my nipples. Once, I tried to touch myself as the hands were, but the minute I moved my arms, the hands faded away. So now I leave my arms at my sides and let the hands have their way with me.

They stroke and caress, and tonight they add a little scratch. Nails. The fingers have nails that rake over my flesh, leaving little red tracks. It feels really good. More sensation. The little ribbons of light pain make my skin tingle and I almost come from that new feeling.

Then the nails scratch their way down my belly to my pussy. As they play with my sopping clit I begin to notice that the hands end in lacy shirt cuffs and royal blue velvet sleeves. Never before have the hands had anything above the wrists. Normally they just fade into nothingness but tonight there are sleeves. And arms.

Hold it. Arms? Then a mouth touches my ear and nibbles on my lobe. "Just go with it, princess," a voice says, carried by hot breath. I shiver, wanting to turn and see what's going on, yet reluctant to end the pleasure. The pleasure wins.

The hands, and arms now, grasp me beneath my thighs and lift me just enough for something wonderfully strong and hard to slip beneath me. Then I see legs, with a sprinkling of dark hair, and shoulders, broad and muscular, naked arms ending in hands, wonderful, expert hands. It's too dark to see more deeply into the room so I can't see a face, if there is one, behind me. However, I know that I'm sitting on someone's lap, still facing the mirror, and hands are playing with my opening.

Then something else is between my legs. Hard and long. The hands push gently on the small of my back until I'm leaning forward. Then my hips are lifted and I'm impaled on the most wonderful instrument of pleasure I've ever felt. Oh, it hurts for a moment, but then it is pure pleasure. Ecstasy.

The hands lift and lower me so I'm being fucked by that fabulous instrument. Eventually the pleasure becomes too much and I climax.

Exhausted, I fall forward and end up on the carpet at my mysterious lover's feet. Finally, when my breathing calms enough to speak, I ask, "Who are you?"

"I'm your prince," he says, "soon to be your husband. My emissaries spoke to your father and he gave me leave to court you. I thought I'd let my mirror help you realize that there's no one for you but me."

"I don't even know you."

"For the moment you know all you need to know. I suggest that we will soon be able to spend a while getting to know each other, but right off we know an important thing about each other. The sex is terrific."

"Are you real, here, now?"

"Yes, and no. The hands are mine, but they aren't here in this room. Neither is this body. But make no mistake, I can pleasure you and, in turn, you can pleasure me."

I sigh. "God, you do pleasure me."

"Then let's move on from here. I'll warn you in advance that I'm not a handsome prince, just an ordinary-looking one, but I'm someone who will love you and please you forever."

I purr.

"I'll arrive at the castle tomorrow and then we'll start to plan our life together. And every night, when I'm in my room on the other side of the castle and you are in yours, I'll come to you this way. At least until our wedding, when I can do it in person."

I smile. "Sounds like a plan."

# Ride 'em, Cowboy

*I* WAS SITTING ON THE EDGE OF MY BED IN MY BRA AND panties, about to put on my stockings, when my husband walked out of the bathroom dressed in his Halloween costume. He loved to ride horses so we'd sort of put together an outfit out of his jeans, chaps, a plaid flannel shirt, a red bandanna and a leather vest. He had on the Western-style boots he wore when he rode horses on the weekend. We'd also gotten a huge twenty-gallon hat and a toy gun belt with two "six-shooters" from one of those party stores, and he'd made a lasso from a length of soft nylon rope. "Gee haa," he said, swinging the rope over his head.

Collin is about six foot three and, at least in my mind, very handsome. He made a great-looking cowboy. "You look wonderful," I told him, trying to get excited about the costume party we were about to attend. Neither of us wanted to go to this silly party but it was a neighborhood thing and sort of a command performance. We were new in the area and both wanted to try to fit in. "Like a real cowboy."

Collin heaved a big sigh and swung the rope again, then flipped it in my direction so it wrapped itself around me at about the middle of my upper arms. "You can be my li'l heifer," he said, trying to create a Western twang.

"Oh, please," I said, rolling my eyes.

"Well, I've got you roped; maybe it's time to rassle you to the ground and brand you."

"Maybe not," I said, wiggling to free myself. Instead of loosening the rope, Collin tightened it and flipped another length around me. Kidding, I said, "I didn't know you were into bondage."

There was a sudden light in his eyes and my pussy reacted immediately. Let me say right now that we're a pretty open-minded pair, and in the two years we've been married we've been pretty experimental. Never anything like this, however. Was he just playing, I wondered, or . . . ?

"Okay, Tex," I said, "enough."

"Really?" Collin said in a suggestive tone.

Suddenly my throat closed and I couldn't say a thing.

He quickly looped another length of rope around my arms and torso and tied the end off. The rope was soft and didn't really hurt, but my elbows were tightly tied to my waist. Now totally serious, with a hot, hungry gleam in his eyes, he rounded the bed and pushed me onto my back. "You're all mine now," he drawled, sounding really silly. However, I didn't laugh. This was too serious.

"I guess I am," I said, softly.

He lifted me slightly and swiveled my body until I was stretched out on the bed, arms still fixed to my sides. Without another word he pulled the bandanna from his neck and tied my ankles together. When he was done, he stood back and looked down at me. "God, you're so sexy like that."

I couldn't think of anything to say. My brain had become like glue. All I could focus on was the heat in my pussy and the tightness of my nipples.

He sat on the bed beside me, cupped my face with both his large hands and pressed his mouth against mine. The kiss was deep, hot and filled with expectations. I love the way he kisses, and we spent long moments exploring the depths of each other's mouths. I wanted to hold him, but kept being reminded of my bound state. Collin nibbled his way along my jawline and nipped my earlobe with his strong, white teeth. Then his lips moved down my neck and out across my shoulder, leaving a string of light, tingling bite marks in his wake.

His hands found my breasts, covered only by the satin of my bra, a length of rope beneath their swell. "You're really hot," he said, tweaking my hard, erect nipples. Then he fastened his teeth onto one bud and bit down until I was panting. My "oh" was followed by a long exhalation. He knows my body so well, and being slightly helpless only added to my excitement. He worked on my tits until the cups of my bra were sopping wet.

When he straightened again, he slowly shook his head. "Too many clothes." After he'd stripped down to his jeans he gazed down at me. "You too."

I shrugged. What could I do?

Collin disappeared and I heard him rummaging around in the kitchen. Then he returned with a large pair of kitchen shears. "This should do the trick. Then we'll get on with the festivities."

I smiled but held my tongue. The last thing I wanted to do was break the mood with a lame joke.

He snicked the scissors menacingly, then cut the center of my bra and parted the fabric, revealing my almost painfully aroused breasts. He knelt beside the bed and played, kissed, bit and licked my tits until I was writhing, needing more. "Baby, God, you're making me crazy," I groaned.

"That makes two of us," he said, his voice hoarse and sexy.

I wanted to hold him, stroke him, urge him onward, but my arms were still immobilized. I would just have to let him set the pace.

He rocked back, then snicked the scissors again. Without another word he cut up the sides of my panties, and with a little wiggling we managed to remove them.

My ankles were still fastened together so he pushed my feet up so they were against my buttocks and pressed my knees apart. The position was a little awkward but in my state of arousal it was all terrific.

I kept my legs in that position as his fingers found my pubic hair and slid through it to my clit. "Baby, you're so wet," he purred. "I'll bet I could shove anything into you right now."

I told you we have an active sex life and we have a nice collection of sex toys. He opened the toy drawer and found the biggest dildo we had, one we've never actually used because it looked too large, both thick and long. "Let's see whether this will work."

"I don't know about that," I said, a bit intimidated.

"We'll stop whenever you want." He knelt beside the bed and rubbed the head of the flesh-colored rod against my wetness. Then he slowly inserted it. Inch by inch it easily filled me. Then, when it was fully inside me, Collin flicked my clit with his tongue. I screamed as orgasm rocked me. I could feel the clench of my vaginal muscles against the plastic toy as my hips bucked.

He kept lightly licking my still-erect clit and it was as though the spasms wouldn't stop. "Baby, be inside me," I cried.

Collin stripped, untied my ankles and pulled the dildo out. He lifted my legs over his shoulders and thrust his hard cock into me. It was like one orgasm blended into the next and in short order, he bellowed and, with a final shove, came.

Later he untied me and we showered together, giggling like we'd just played with a new toy. Actually I guess we had. We arrived at the party only an hour late and just grinned and looked at each other when asked why. I think we're now labeled the sexiest couple in the neighborhood. Ride 'em, cowboy. Gee haa.

# Dracula's Cape

"Nice to meet you, Marcy."

"Nice to meet you too, Devin," I said. The room was filled
with hockey players, eighteenth-century women, ballerinas and
even a court jester. "This is quite a party."

"A costume party. Really. It is a bit much, don't you think?"
Devin asked. We stood to one side, near the bar. He was dressed
in a vampire costume, tight black bodysuit, fabulously huge
cape with a large cowl, and a pair of fangs large enough that
not even Dracula himself could have totally closed his mouth.
He wasn't terribly attractive, but he had a spark in his eyes that
added to his natural charm.

"I'll admit that it really is silly," I said, "but the people are
so nice. And I got to meet you." I looked from his costume to
mine. I was dressed as his opposite, an angel, with white wings,
a gauzy dress, with white, thigh-high stockings and white ballet

slippers. "We make quite a pair—sort of yin and yang." I was actually flirting. How great did that feel. . . .

"Just what I was thinking," Devin said, his smile revealing more of his fangs.

"Oh look, there are Collin and Danielle. They live down the street," I said, to try to cut the sexual tension a little. "I didn't think they were going to show." They were dressed as cowboy and cowgirl.

"And look at the grins on their faces," Devin said. "We know what kept them, I'll bet," he continued with a leer.

I looked at the couple and they looked radiant, with little, secretive smiles on their faces. "You're really evil," I said. "You're not supposed to notice things like that."

"Why not? I'm just being realistic. A little nookie must have held them up."

"Not such a bad thing," I said. As I listened to what I'd just said, it sounded like quite an invitation. Did I mean it that way? He was so sexy.

"Right you are, my dear," Devin said, using a thick Dracula accent. Then he leaned over and scratched my neck with his fangs. With the tip of his tongue he licked little circles on my carotid artery.

"Mmm," I purred, feeling as though I'd been captured by Dracula's spell. "Nice. Very nice."

Holding the sides of his cape in his hands, he wrapped his arms around me, enclosing me in the folds. As he held me close he moved his feet as though we were dancing to the strains of music coming from the CD player. The room was lit with only candles, many of which were stuck inside pumpkins, and the walls were covered with spooky decorations. Shadows danced everywhere.

I allowed him to press his body full against mine and couldn't miss the large bulge at the front of his bodysuit. Damn, I was hot and hungry. What the hell? We were in public after all. What could happen?

We spent a few minutes rubbing bodies, undulating against each other, his hot breath on my neck. "I want to get you in private," he growled against my ear.

"Just like that?" I said.

"Just like that."

"You're moving a bit too fast for me," I admitted.

"Okay, how about right here?" He left the cape draped over my shoulders and slipped his hands down my back. He kneaded my buttocks through the lightweight fabric of my costume, pressing his erection hard against my belly. He moved his hips so that he was actually masturbating in the middle of my friend's living room. His fingers slipped between my cheeks and reached deep between my legs, just barely reaching the back of my slit.

"I can feel your heat," he said, fingering the crotch of my panties. "Does the idea of doing this in public turn you on?"

A single nod showed my inability to respond coherently to his words.

"Good." While one hand continued to play with my ass, the other found my breast through the gauzy fabric of my costume. Because of the cut of the dress I had not been able to wear a bra. I have quite a bit of natural uplift so I decided to go with that look. "Oh, look what I found," he said, squeezing one nipple.

"Cut that out," I said, not really meaning a word of it.

"Riiight," he said, squeezing a bit harder. My breasts have always been the center of my sexuality. I love to be fucked, have my pussy licked and such, but my tits are where it's at for me. It's as though there's an electrically charged wire running from my tits right to my clit. He obviously sensed that and he began to establish a rhythm to his pinches. It was as though I were being fucked. Beneath Dracula's cape. Right there in the middle of the living room.

My knees were weak and threatened to buckle. "Don't let it happen," he whispered in my ear. "Then everyone will know."

I locked my knees in an effort to remain standing, moving my feet just enough to seem to be dancing. Fortunately it was pretty dark.

Slowly his fingers began to pull my dress up in the back. When it was all bunched in his hand, he tucked it into the back of my panties, then began to explore beneath the elastic of the leg holes.

"God, you're so wet," he said. He moved his hand to my belly beneath the dress and slipped his fingers down the front of my undies. He lost no time in finding my clit and he rubbed it in the rhythm I craved. I was going to come. Right here. His thumb took up the caresses while his fingers delved in my crease.

Beneath the cape he stroked my most private parts until, jaws clamped together so I wouldn't scream, I climaxed.

"Outside. In my car. Now," he said and I shakily followed him out the door into the warm evening air.

He opened the back door of his SUV and we climbed onto the flat rear seat. He pulled the front of his costume aside and, pushing me onto my back, rammed his cock into me. I wrapped my legs around his waist as he pounded over and over until, with a roar, he came. He rubbed my clit until I joined him, climaxing for a second time.

Panting, we lay crumpled on the seat, too weak to move.

"Shit, that was dynamite," he said.

I could only nod. We must have dozed for a while; then I came to and looked at my watch. "Shit. Honey. We need to head home. We've got to have the babysitter home in fifteen minutes."

I felt his deep sigh. "Okay. And let's do this again. It's fun to pretend not to know each other. It's like we were dating all over again."

I sighed with him. "It's tough with kids, but we do manage to keep it fresh."

"We do," he said. "And after I drive that girl home, I'll meet you in the bedroom, my little angel."

"Last one to the bed is a rotten vampire."

# The Bad Girl

"**H**AVE YOU BEEN A BAD GIRL TODAY?" ANNA'S HUSBAND, Sam, asked as he dropped his briefcase on the hall table.

Those words caused Anna's entire body to suddenly tingle all over. She caught on immediately and knew exactly what Sam was suggesting—a night of great sex. He already knew that the kids were spending the night at Anna's parents' house and, from the slight tenting of his khakis, she realized that he'd obviously been thinking about the evening to come all the way home from work. She smiled teasingly, lowered her head and stared at her Nikes. "Maybe."

"Come on, Anna, fess up." When she remained silent, he said, "Okay, let's see. Did you pick up my shirts at the laundry?"

"Yes," she said and pointed to the neatly folded stack of dress shirts on the dining room table. On her way home from her day of substitute teaching at the local elementary school, she'd stopped and retrieved his shirts as she did each Friday. Then she'd gotten the boys from the school bus and dropped them at her parents' house for an overnight visit.

"But you didn't put them away, now, did you?" he said, his voice deep and stern.

Usually he wouldn't have mentioned it, but rather he'd merely pick up the stack of shirts on the way into the bedroom of their small suburban split-level, and put them in his dresser drawer. But he was quick on the uptake and had quickly fixed on her first transgression. When they started playing their game she used to say that she'd been bad, but now he liked to catch her at some silly, created sin. "I'm sorry," she said, her voice small. She listened to herself and worried that she was overacting, but he seemed content with her subservient attitude.

He raised an eyebrow and stared at her as she peeked up at him through her lashes. "Is that the only thing you've been bad about?" He cocked his head to one side and it was all Anna could do not to giggle, or kiss him.

"Yes," she whispered, getting further into the swing of the evening. God, he looked so sexy with that *"I'm so hot for your body but I'm going to play this game all the way"* look in his deep brown eyes. "I've been really good today." But her mind was already racing to find ways to magnify her "punishment." She felt her pussy throb at the erotic visions dancing through her mind.

"Is dinner ready?" he asked, his voice hard but his eyes gleaming with sensuality.

"It will be on the table in ten minutes."

"Well, then, I guess your punishment will have to wait until after dinner."

Anna loved the anticipation almost as much as she enjoyed the hot sex they always had when Sam was in this mood, and she knew that Sam was looking forward to later as much as she was.

They'd met nine years before on a checkout line at the local Kmart. The cash register had run out of paper tape and it had taken a visit from a supervisor to get a new roll threaded properly. When she'd muttered that it always happened to her, Sam had chimed in that, actually, it was his karma, not hers, that caused the problem. They'd gotten to chatting and they had both felt an immediate chemistry, and on their third date they'd discovered how hot lovemaking could be. Eleven months later they'd gotten married, and a year after Mike joined their family, followed in eighteen months by Jake.

For a while when both the boys were at home, toddling, getting into trouble, sapping all their energy, their sex life had gone to hell in a handcart. Once the boys were in school, however, with lots of help from magazine articles, their friends and their own creativity, their sex life had soared. Several months before, they'd stumbled on their mutual love of a little pain with their pleasure, and now it was as if they were newlyweds. Well, not newlyweds exactly, since they now knew so much about each other's hot buttons that they could turn the heat even higher than when they were new at it.

Anna put Sam's shirts in his dresser, then dished up his

favorite meal: lamb chops and macaroni and cheese. As she handed him his plate she thought about being a "bad girl," and slopped a little pasta into his lap.

"I think you did that on purpose," Sam said, his eyes twinkling. "That was very naughty."

"I know and I'm sorry," she said softly. Sorry, my foot, she thought. It was all she could do not to grin.

"Not half as sorry as you'll be later," he said, rubbing his palm as if he already felt the tingle after several swats on her behind. "For now, you get to think about your punishment. I wonder what I should use: my hand"—he paused for effect—"or something new."

Something new? Did he have a surprise in his briefcase? Recently he'd started to do a little shopping on the net and he'd have a toy sent to him at his office, then surprise her. Thank heavens for plain brown wrapping.

During dinner she could barely get her brain or body to function. What did he have in mind for later? Throughout their meal she tried to respond to Sam's small talk about his day at work and hers but the primary thing occupying her mind was her "punishment." "Earth to Anna," Sam said when she'd been silent for several minutes. "You're not paying attention. That's another black mark against you, you know."

"I guess so." Anna's hands were actually shaking as she wielded her knife and fork, scooping the last forkful of macaroni into her mouth. It tasted like bland goo and she struggled to swallow, wriggling in her chair, unable to get comfortable. As she moved, she was aware that her pussy was juicy and twitchy.

"Let's just stack the dishes in the sink for tonight," Sam suggested, "and get on with *things*."

The way he said *things* made her nerves jangle deliciously.

A few minutes later Sam settled on the living room sofa with Anna standing in front of him. "Okay, let's review. You didn't put my shirts away, you spilled mac and cheese in my lap and you didn't pay proper attention to the conversation at dinner. Is there anything else?"

"No."

"All right, why don't you get my briefcase and let's see what's inside."

With trembling hands, Anna fetched her husband's case and set it on the floor beside his feet. When he patted the cushion next to him, she settled, not touching him. He wrapped his arm around her shoulders and said, slipping out of character for a few moments, "You know I would never hurt you, except in fun, don't you?"

She too changed from the subservient wife into the life partner she truly was. "Of course."

"And you know that all you have to do is holler *uncle* and everything will stop."

"I do. What's up?"

"I did a little surfing a few days ago and found something that really turned me on. But if it's not your thing . . ."

"Stop with the disclaimers. I know how to call things off. What did you get?"

He picked up his case and set it on his lap. Flipping the catch, he opened the lid and took out a large, flat package in a plain brown box. "Open it."

She found the tear strip and pulled. Out poured several brightly colored pages of advertisements and a large, rectangular paddle. "Would this be okay with you?"

She smiled. She'd suspected as much and had already done some thinking about whether she was ready to play this way. She wasn't sure, but she had complete trust in Sam. They could start but she knew he'd stop immediately if she hollered *uncle*. She gazed into his sexy brown eyes and nodded.

He took the paddle and rubbed its smooth, highly polished, wooden surface over the palm of his hand. "You've been very naughty."

Anna lowered her head and slipped back into character. In a tiny voice she said, "I know and I'm very sorry."

Sam frowned. "Sorry isn't enough. Drop your jeans."

She knew the drill, quickly removed her jeans and stood in front of him in her tee shirt and panties. "Let's try the first few with your panties on," Sam said, patting his thighs.

Anna draped herself over them, pink nylon–covered bottom in the air. "Please don't hurt me," she said, continuing the drama.

"I have to hurt you for your own good. You need to learn to be more attentive to my needs."

She giggled. "Oh, I'll be attentive to your needs, all right," she said in her natural voice.

Sam swatted her bottom with the paddle. "Don't get smart with me, young lady."

Anna had barely felt the smack but the sound made her jump. "Ow," she said, reflexively.

Sam adjusted her position on his lap and as she moved, his

hard erection pushed against her hip. He was obviously as hot as she was. Again he brought the paddle down on her bottom, a little harder this time. It stung, the sensation traveling quickly to her pussy. She felt her lips swell and her body open. Again he smacked her ass. And again. And again.

"That's five," Sam said, stroking her bottom gently with the wood. "Have you learned your lesson yet?"

"Oh yes," she blurted out.

"You said that much too quickly, without any thought. I think that calls for five more. On your bare ass this time." He yanked her panties and, with her help, pulled them down to her ankles.

With the first light spank on her bare skin, he reached under her shirt and unclasped her bra. Then he reached beneath her and flipped it up out of the way. He rubbed his palm over her already-hard nipple. "Makes you hot, doesn't it?" he purred.

"God yes," she said.

"Then let's cool you down a little." He swatted her ass hard.

That hurt, but it was somehow terribly exciting as the pain flashed to her cunt. She wriggled against Sam's hard cock, still imprisoned in his slacks. One more hard spank and she'd had enough. She realized that any more would cease to be exciting. "Uncle," she whispered.

He smoothed his palm over her heated ass and tweaked her nipple. "I don't think I could have held out much longer either. Last one to the bedroom . . ."

In only moments they were naked and Sam was sliding his

hard cock deep into her soaked channel. Each thrust of his rigid shaft caused her ass to press into the sheets and a small spear of pain/pleasure echoed through her. She wrapped her legs around Sam's waist and linked her ankles, pushing upward as he thrust.

It took only a few minutes before, with his customary roar, Sam came deep inside her. Then he slipped his fingers between them and rubbed Anna's clit until, with a scream, she climaxed as well.

They collapsed together and dozed, Anna looking forward to the next time the kids were gone and to finding some transgressions of Sam's.

# *Her Perfect Lover*

$\mathscr{L}$ORD, SHE FELT GOOD. TOBOR WAS THE PERFECT LOVER
and the fact that she had to enjoy him secretly during the afternoon didn't change that. Since she telecommuted on Wednesdays it was easy.

Now she sat at her computer, typing the reports her boss
would expect her to finish. Ms. Sanderford didn't care when she
got them done, as long as when she went into the office on Thurs-
day her work was complete. And it always was.

As she labored Tobor had been sitting patiently in a chair in
the third bedroom of the house she shared with her husband,
the one they'd made over into a little office. Finally he looked at
her and said, "You look like you're almost finished with what
you're doing. If you've reached a stopping place . . ." He didn't
complete the sentence.

She delayed gratification as long as she could, then said, "I think I can stop now, Tobor."

"Good," he purred, his voice soft and melodious. "Shall I pour some bubbly?"

"I think that would be lovely," she said. Anything to heighten the excitement of her afternoon delight.

He withdrew a bottle of champagne from the tiny fridge behind the dresser and with sure, deft movements proceeded to uncork it, and she was rewarded with a delightful pop. As he poured she watched his hands. He had such graceful hands, with long fingers, well-manicured nails and wide palms. She loved watching his hands, thinking of them later, playing familiar melodies over her body.

He handed her the glass—he never had any himself—and she sipped. It was cool with just a little yeasty taste. She rolled the second sip around in her mouth, letting the wine wet each part, savoring the taste.

"You look a little tense," Tobor said. "How about a neck rub?" He didn't wait for her answer but walked around behind her chair and used those fabulous hands to massage away her tension. He seemed to know exactly how hard to push, how deep to press his thumbs to cause her just a little pain and yet relax her tight shoulder muscles.

She sipped more wine and, when her glass was empty, he refilled it. As he handed back her glass, filled with pale gold liquid, he leaned over and kissed her along her hairline, then her eyes and her cheeks. Lingering over the slowly building throb between her legs, she sat still and let his mouth make love to her.

His lips traveled to her ear and he tickled the inside with the tip of his tongue, then mimicked the motions of fucking. When he blew on the wetness she felt a shiver echo down her spine. He knew exactly how to drive her mad.

He took her free hand and guided her to her feet. Still holding her glass, she wrapped her free arm around his waist and pulled him close. He was so beautiful. She knew that one shouldn't use the word *beautiful* for a man, but he was. His hair was black as ebony, long and lustrous, his eyes almost as dark. He had lashes that any woman would kill for, and bedroom lips. *Bedroom eyes* was the usual expression, but it was his mouth that made her think of long, leisurely lovemaking. Like pictures she saw of Elvis Presley in his heyday. A bedroom mouth.

He pressed it against hers and slipped his tongue between her lips. He sucked lightly on her tongue, then used that fucking motion again with his tongue between her teeth. She wanted his cock in her pussy like that, but she would wait. She could wait. But not too long.

He cupped the back of her head with one of those sexy hands, then used the other to pull her tee shirt from her jeans. His fingers were warm as his hands slid up her ribs and found one of her naked breasts. Yes, she cheated. She wanted his hands on her nipples so badly that she'd stopped wearing a bra on her wonderful Wednesdays.

He did as she knew he would, found her nipple and twisted it lightly, causing just a frisson of pain and pleasure, all curled together. Heat ran through her, causing her tissues to swell and moisten. His mouth was still making love to hers as his fingers did their usual magic with her tit. Her knees trembled and a shudder ran through her.

He knew she could barely stand so he took her wineglass and set it on the table beside her bed, then, almost effortlessly, scooped her up and lay her on the slippery quilt. He yanked up her tee shirt so it bunched under her arms, as if he couldn't wait long enough to pull it off completely, then pressed his face against her breastbone and pressed her large breasts against the sides of his face. Deep in the valley of her cleavage, he kissed her skin while his fingers again found her nipples and squeezed. Her breasts had always been her weak spot.

He turned his face until he could take one hard nipple into his mouth and suckle. She was going crazy with pleasure. His mouth alternated sides until she couldn't keep her hips still. She wanted him so badly.

He quickly removed her jeans and panties. She'd worn new ones today, but she knew he couldn't notice. "You're so beautiful," he told her as he stripped off his clothing. His body was perfectly formed, with a hairless chest, wide shoulders and narrow hips. His cock was a rigid rod, standing out from its nest of dark hair.

But no, not yet. Tobor knew better. He settled between her knees and applied his mouth to her pussy. He took his time, circling her clit yet not touching it until she thought she'd scream. Then, when he finally found her sweet spot, he did a sort of figure eight, first pressing, then leaving. Over and over he teased until she said, "I can't go much longer without you."

He climbed up on his knees and crouched over her, holding his cock for her to admire. "I want it inside me," she said. Sometimes she'd fellate him, but not this time. She was too hungry.

"Your wish . . ."

He plunged into her, ramming himself into her over and over, then finding her clit with his fingers and leaning down to suckle her nipple as she came. The power of her climax was almost like having convulsions, losing control of her entire body as the spasms took her. Long moments later she was still shuddering.

"Honey," she heard a voice call, "I'm home."

She quickly took a breath. "I'll be down in a minute," she called. Then she looked at Tobor. "I'm sorry."

"Don't be," he said.

She rose from the bed and Tobor went back to his chair in the corner. She chuckled at her little joke, thinking of him as Tobor, *robot* spelled backward. With a long sigh, she reached beneath his long hair to the nape of his neck, and switched him off.

## A Few Naughty Ballads for Your Enjoyment

In the Garden of Eden lay Adam
Complacently stroking his madam.
And great was his mirth
For on all of the Earth
There were only two balls and he had 'em.

A woman from North Carolina
Strung violin strings across her vagina.
With the proper-sized cocks
She reliably played Bach's
"Toccata and Fugue" in D minor.

There once was a man from Alsace
Whose balls were constructed of brass.
When he clanged them together

They played "Stormy Weather"
And lightning came out of his ass.


On the breasts of a barmaid in Sale
Is printed the price of the ale.
And on her behind
For the sake of the blind
Is the same information in braille.


There was a young lady from Natchez
Who chanced to be born with two snatches.
And she often said, "Shit,
Why, I'd give my left tit,
For a man with equipment that matches."


There was a young lady named Alice
Who used a dynamite stick for a phallus.
They found her vagina
In North Carolina
And part of her anus in Dallas.


There once was a man from Bel Aire
Who was doing a maid on the stair.
On the thirty-ninth stroke
The banister broke
And he finished her off in midair.


A newlywed couple named Kelly
Awoke one day, belly to belly.

For when they went to bed
They used glue instead
Of good old petroleum jelly.

There once was a gay from Khartoum
Took a lesbian up to his room
And they argued all night
About who had the right
To do what and with which and to whom.

An Argentine gaucho named Bruno
Said, "Sex is the one thing I do know.
Women are fine.
Sheep are divine.
But a llama is numero uno."

An oversexed lady from Norway
Hung by her toes from a doorway.
She called to her beau,
"Come over here, Joe.
I think I've discovered one more way."

There once was a harlot named Prue
Who filled up her cunt with strong glue.
Said she with a grin,
"Well, they paid to get in
They can pay to get out again too!"

There once was a young man from Lear
Who was thrown into jail for a year

For an action obscene
On the very first green
Where the sign says to "Enter course here."

On the bridge stood the young Duke of Buckingham
Thinking of tits and of sucking them,
While observing the stunts
Of the cunts in the punts
And the tricks of the pricks that were fucking them.

# Creativity

*K*EVIN LOVED TO READ EROTIC SHORT STORIES ON THE Web. He had dozens of sites listed in his favorites, and when he got home from work each day at about three in the afternoon, he quickly wiggled his mouse to wake his computer, then moved from site to site to find the most recent additions. He read heterosexual, gay and lesbian stories, tales of hypnotism and mind control, bondage and even occasional sadistic fiction, although for the most part his tastes ran to stories about men and women enjoying erotic interludes, then parting with no strings attached.

He had a really nice wife who satisfied his sexual needs, as he satisfied hers, but his "grand passion" was confined to the Web.

He didn't know exactly when he'd started thinking seriously about writing a story himself but the more he pondered, the more he believed he might just pull it off. He could do this stuff. After all, what was there to it? Most of the tales he read had little real plot, just lots of detailed descriptions of bodies and what they did to each other, and he knew that part as well as anyone else. He had fantasies, so all he had to do was draw on them and bingo, a good story. Maybe he could even get one posted on one of his favorite sites.

He considered writing for several days. Then, one Tuesday afternoon, after an hour of reading, he booted up his seldom-used word processor. Soon the blank page stared back at him, so he put his fingers on the keys and tried to think of a title. Nothing came to him. "Okay," he said aloud, "I'll write the story and think of a title later."

"She was beautiful." *Okay, good start. Let me build her first; then the action can grow from that.* "Long black hair hung to her waist." He loved long hair. "She had deep blue eyes with long dark lashes." He closed his eyes and a small smile curved his lips. Snapping his lids up he banged on the keys. "Her body was lush, with long shapely legs, large, white, pillowy breasts and prominent nipples, a narrow waist and soft hair covering her . . ."

Her what? What words would he use?

"Come on, finish me," a voice said from his computer.

His back straightened and his fingers froze.

"How about *pussy*, *cunt* or *snatch*," the voice said. "If you'll just get on with it, we can get this show on the road."

He was incapable of movement. What the hell was going on? Had he accidentally triggered some recording from iTunes? He slowly clenched and unclenched his fingers and then clicked around the windows he had open. No, nothing seemed to be playing.

"That's useless. You won't find me there. Just finish what you're writing and you'll understand."

He clicked back to the word processor. "soft hair covering her . . ." He typed the word *pussy*.

Suddenly she was there. In the room. She was just as he'd described her, large eyes, long hair. Naked, gloriously, fabulously naked, with soft hair covering her . . . pussy.

"Phew. It took you long enough," she said. "Okay, blow job, anal, a little slapping around? What's your pleasure?"

Finally he found his voice. "What . . ."

"I guess you're pretty new to this. Okay, I'll explain as much as I know. Do you really think all those folks who write erotica do it for the solo kicks? Oh, some do, of course. Some write with one hand on the keyboard and one in their laps; that's for sure."

Kevin quickly made sure both his hands were on the keyboard instead of one in his lap, as it often was while he read.

She went on. "Others eventually find girls—or guys, of course, if that's their thing—like me. How long have you been writing?"

"This was to be my first story," Kevin said, barely able to gather his wits. He realized that his knees were shaking.

"You're kidding," she said. "It usually takes dozens or even hundreds of stories before someone like me appears. You're very lucky."

"You just appear?" This had to be some kind of elaborate joke. It couldn't be real. It just couldn't.

"I don't know the exact details. All I know is that as long as your story stays on the hard drive of your computer—" She burst out laughing. "Hard drive, get it? *Hard* drive."

As laughter rippled over her, her large breasts jiggled. He became aware that she was totally unconcerned about her lack of clothing. "Anyway," she continued, "as long as this story stays in your computer you can bring me up anytime." She laughed again. "And I can get you up too."

"Keep the story?" He was annoyed that he couldn't get any more coherent thoughts through his brain.

"Sure. You can refine it anytime, change my hair or eyes, more fully describe my pussy, whatever you want. Then you can write any action you've ever wanted."

Slowly the thought that this might just be real began to take over his brain, and he felt his cock stiffen. He had a satisfying sex life as it was, but this was his golden opportunity. His wife was pretty good at oral sex, but she couldn't deep throat without gagging. Maybe . . .

"Type it and it shall be done," she said, her voice lowering and sounding breathy and hot. "Just type something, love."

"What's in this for you?"

"You mean why do I do it? I get to get out of that word processor from time to time and I get to have good sex."

"That's it?"

"That's pretty much it."

Kevin checked the time on his screen. At least an hour before Lissa got home from work. "Okay, I'll bite." Kevin decided to try it out with something nonsexual first. "She had a thick Southern accent," he typed.

"Well, sugar," she said, honey dripping from her lips, "that was a tiny, little ole start."

It had worked. His cock had swelled with each line he typed but he was afraid to give this thing the ultimate test. "She had deep, red lips." When he looked up it was true. "And her name was Gwen."

"Sure enough, sugar, Gwen it is."

Okay, this was it. He parted his knees and slid his hips forward on the swivel chair. "She crouched between his spread knees and stroked him."

And she was there, long, soft fingers taking his almost painfully swollen cock from beneath his shorts. She wrapped her hand around him and slowly slid her palm from tip to base. She kept stroking until he thought he was ready to burst.

Then he realized. He needed to continue the story. "She parted her red lips and took him in her mouth."

Oh God, it was so good. Her breath was hot and wet as she engulfed him, sliding her red lips over his skin, taking most of the length of him into her mouth. Then she held still. With quaking hands he reached his keyboard. "She sucked him, giving him the best head he'd ever had."

In and out, up and down, until he was ready to spurt. But he couldn't. He just kept getting higher and higher but it was as though his cock were stuck. The pleasure was tremendous, but he was becoming frustrated. "She let him come in her mouth," he typed and he exploded, collapsing back onto his chair, as she faded away, saying softly, "Until next time, sugar."

It had been wonderful, but so dispassionate. There was no feeling, no caring, no cuddling afterward. Okay, men weren't supposed to like to cuddle after sex, but he liked pressing his spent body against his wife's back, cradling her buttocks against his flaccid cock.

He would refine the story, hone the action until he had the sex exactly the way he wanted it. But where would the surprises be? He liked it when his wife rolled over and encouraged him to take her doggie style, or when she slapped him on the ass or masturbated him. He never knew exactly what sex would be like and he enjoyed that thoroughly.

"Hi, babe," his wife called; then the front door slammed behind her. "What's up? How was your day at work? I brought KFC. I hope that's okay. You get to fetch tomorrow."

He loved the little sounds she made as she came and the way she occasionally bit him on the ear just for fun. Kevin hesitated, his finger over the "save" key. He took a deep breath as his wife wandered into the bedroom, dropped onto the bed and pulled off her shoes. "Did you decide to write your story?" she asked. "I think you'll really be good at it."

"You think so?" he asked as she rubbed the arches of her feet.

She giggled. "Sure. All you have to do is write about some night we've spent. I know women would envy me. That's for sure."

Kevin's finger moved slightly and he pushed the button to close the word processor. DO YOU WISH TO EXIT WITHOUT SAVING YOUR WORK?

He clicked "yes" and the word processor closed. As the screen changed he thought he heard a small squawk, then nothing.

## Special Services

I WENT TO THE MASSAGE PARLOR FOR HELP FOR MY BACK. Okay, okay, I hear you. It's like saying you read *Playboy* for the articles, but in this case it's the truth.

I've had a bad back for years, and several days before "the incident," as I think of it, I'd done some lifting that I shouldn't have. I should have known better, but I will admit that I screwed up—and for three days my back had been steadily worsening. That morning I'd barely made it out of bed and only ten minutes under a hot shower had allowed me to function.

I'd been complaining to several of my friends at work and a few of them recommended "Fulmer Building Therapeutic Massages," a place that specialized in massages for medicinal purposes. Since chiropractic care isn't covered under my medical plan and this seemed to be considerably cheaper, I decided to give it a try.

The place seemed very upscale, with an entrance on the ground floor of a high-rise office building in Midtown, within walking distance of my office. It had a discreet, tasteful sign on the door that was small but not totally hidden. The waiting room was decorated with the kind of stuff you find in doctor's offices: squarish furniture, subdued lighting and low tables covered with well-thumbed magazines. A few people waited— mixed genders—so I relaxed, now convinced that the place was on the up-and-up. It's not that I don't trust the guys at work, you understand, but—well, I don't trust the guys at work.

I checked in with the receptionist, a professional-looking woman of indeterminate age, and told her about my back problems. She looked me over thoroughly, nodded sympathetically and quoted me a price for an hour's treatment. The price was high, but not exorbitant. When I agreed and had filled out the paperwork, she took my credit card and ran it through her computer. After a few minutes she told me someone would be able to help me in a short while.

I sat down gingerly and thumbed through several week-old issues of *Business Week* until the door to the rest of the office opened and I heard someone call my name. "I'm Dale Randall," I said, carefully getting to my feet.

Another nice-looking woman held the door open for me. "Nice to meet you, Mr. Randall," she said, her voice cultured and soft. "I'm sorry to hear about your muscle spasms. Ellen will be able to help you, I'm sure." She showed me into a small room with a massage table in the center, a sink on one side and a small curtained area in one corner. "You'll find gowns in the bin. Put it on with the opening in the front." She paused in a spiel she'd probably done hundreds of times, then continued. "It would make things easier if you would remove all your clothing so Ellen will have access to all your back muscles. If you prefer, however, you can leave your shorts on along with whatever else makes you most comfortable. We certainly don't want you tense."

After she closed the door behind her I found one of those gowns you get in doctors' offices in a little plastic sleeve. Very professional. I've never been nervous about being nude, so I stripped and put the gown on. It was only a few moments until I heard a soft knock at the door. "Yes," I said.

The masseuse walked in. She was of medium height, with a slender build, short, brown curly hair and lovely deep brown eyes. She was wearing a short-sleeved white blouse and black slacks. I couldn't help but notice her arms. They were smooth, but very muscular. She must do a lot of massages.

"Good afternoon, Mr. Randall. I'm Ellen and I'll be trying to help you today. I understand you've got some back issues." She ran water in the sink and washed her hands with plenty of soap.

"Call me Dale," I said; then, as she dried her hands and arms, I told her about my back. While I spoke she spread a large towel over the table and arranged a small one over the headrest.

"Let's begin with your back, although as you might know, many back problems originate from the abdominal muscles as well."

I lay facedown on the table and she adjusted the headrest until I was really comfortable. Then she began. She pulled up the back of the gown and stroked my flesh. Her touch was both professional and erotic, but I squelched any sexual thoughts. She pressed on a few locations on my spine and I told her exactly where it hurt.

"Okay," she said, "I've got a pretty good picture of what's going on. We've got plenty of time, so I'm going to begin with your legs and arms, just to get your muscles as relaxed as I can before I go to work on your back and shoulders."

She had great hands. I quickly forgot about the erotic stimulation and concentrated on her fingers as they worked over my limbs. After about ten minutes I was totally limp. Then she massaged my shoulders and back. Although I didn't move I realized that my back did feel much better. As she moved on to my buttocks I wondered why there, but since she'd been really helping, I didn't ask.

As her hands kneaded my cheeks, all my erotic thoughts came flooding back. Her fingers slipped into my butt crack and I could feel my cock getting harder. Fortunately I was lying on my stomach so I assumed that she wasn't aware.

Her talented fingers slipped farther forward between my thighs, and the tips found my sac. *She'd better stop,* I thought, *before something more happens,* but instead of telling her, I reveled in the sensuality. At that point I was still sure she was unaware of my plight.

"If you'd like to turn over, I can work on your abs," she said, her voice gentle and professional.

Hmm. Dilemma. If I turned over, it would be impossible to

hide my erection. However, I glanced at the clock on the wall and saw that it had been only half an hour. I was entitled to a full hour and I assumed that she'd seen erections before. I was sure she'd caused more than a few. I could, of course, ask her to just work on my back, but . . . I turned over, trying to keep the edges of the gown over my hard-on.

No use. She saw my problem immediately. She chuckled softly, then raised a questioning eyebrow. "I see your problem, and we can just ignore it while I try to fix your abdominals. Or . . ."

I knew immediately what her *or* meant, and right then I didn't think I was mentally ready for it. "Let's see whether my abs will help my back," I said, trying to sound disinterested in the rest of what she was offering.

She nodded and smiled. "I totally understand." She coated her hands with oil, rubbed them together and went to work on my belly. She pressed deep into the soft flesh, and each time she ventured below my belly button my cock twitched and grew. Slowly I began to hope she'd make her offer again, but she became quite careful. I thought about the cop shows I'd seen on TV and realized that if I suggested something and if I were a cop, she could say she'd been entrapped. God, every motion of her hands made me want more.

"Uh," I said. "If . . ."

"Did you want something more?" she asked, looking totally innocent. She "accidentally" bumped her wrist against my cock.

"God, yes."

"What would you like?" she said, I guess needing me to spell it out.

"My erection is making me crazy. Can you help?" I said.

"You are saying that you want me to help you come?"

"Oh, yes."

"We're really not that sort of establishment, but if you're sure that's what you want . . ."

"Yes," I hissed.

"There will be an extra charge for *special services.*"

"I assumed that."

"Good."

As I watched she poured a pool of oil into her palm and slowly, oh so slowly, rubbed her hands together. Now that I had committed to a hand job, I was eager for it to begin. But she was moving so slowly. So slowly. When I glanced at her face I saw her watching me with a small smile. "We can't rush these things, can we?"

She rubbed my upper thighs; then her thumbs dug into the muscles beside my sac. I thought I couldn't get any harder but each push drove my cock farther upward. She scratched my balls with her short nails, then wrapped her fingers around my shaft. Base to tip, then tip to base. Then, she made a tube of her fingers and started at the head and pressed to the base. When her hand got far enough down the shaft, she duplicated the motion with the other. Over and over she used first one hand, then the other to create an endless vagina.

It felt so good that I wanted it to last. Not a chance. After only a few moments streams of goo spurted from my cock. "The best relaxation there is," she purred, "for your back and the rest of you."

She wet a small towel with warm water from the sink and

slowly cleaned me up. "I hope I've fixed your problems," Ellen said softly, "and if you ever need any more help of any kind, please ask for me."

Massage parlor indeed. Wow.

Oh, and my back feels great.

## More Special Services

$\mathscr{I}$ DON'T THINK I'D HAVE HAD THE NERVE TO MAKE MY
first appointment with Ellen had I known what kind of massage
was possible, but once I had, I was hooked. I'd seen the charge
for the "Fulmer Building Therapeutic Massage" on my credit
card slip, then an additional one labeled "FBTM Special Services." Special services indeed. It had certainly been well worth
the extra charge.

I thought about my visit for several days. My back was, indeed, much improved, as was my disposition. I had never told
the guys who'd suggested the place that I'd actually made the
appointment, so I didn't have to explain anything to them. I
wondered whether they knew what kind of special services were
available. Each time I saw one of the guys it was all I could do
not to grin but, although I wanted to share my experience and
ask them about theirs, I knew I couldn't talk about it with a

straight face. I'd been to a massage parlor, a hot, erotic massage parlor. Holy shit.

I couldn't get the afternoon out of my mind, and just a week later I called for another appointment with Ellen. The wait seemed interminable, but it was also glorious. Knowing what was going to happen was almost as great as the actuality. My second visit was as good as the first. By my third visit she got me off quickly, then gave me a full-body massage until I was ready to come again. And I did, with her help.

As I changed back into my clothes after my fourth or fifth visit, always at five on Fridays, I glanced in the mirror and thought I saw something move. I looked behind me but there was nothing there. Ellen was washing the table and I looked at her questioningly. It couldn't be, could it? "Is someone watching us from behind that mirror?"

"Of course not," she said too quickly, suddenly blushing furiously.

I considered, then said, "I think the idea of being watched is pretty kinky." I walked over to her and placed her hand on the hard bulge beneath my zipper. I was again erect despite my previous orgasm. "Tell me truthfully, is someone watching us?"

She lowered her eyes and nodded slightly.

"Every time?"

She still looked embarrassed that she'd been found out, but she seemed a little comforted by the fact that I said I might enjoy watching. "Not every time, but when we have someone in here for our special services and if there's someone interested in witnessing that sort of thing, we let him or her watch. There's no harm done. Please, don't say anything. Except for those who participate, no one is supposed to know."

I ignored her. "Do customers pay for the privilege?"

She nodded again.

"Could I watch someone?"

Her head snapped up. "You?"

"Me," I said. "It's always been an interest of mine—watching, that is. Is there much of an extra charge?"

Slowly a smile lightened her face. "There's only a small one," she said.

It was probably a lousy thing to do, spying on someone getting his rocks off, but the idea made me so hot. And anyway everyone involved was doing something illegal.

"How would it work?"

"We have other customers like you who come pretty regularly for special services." *Come.* We both laughed at her double entendre. "You know what I mean. We could set something up for you."

"I'd like that."

"Would you like me to be there watching with you or would you take care of things on your own?"

"I think I can handle it myself," I said, laughing at yet another double entendre. "And I'll see you again another time for a massage." I was getting to be quite a regular.

Ellen had obviously told the receptionist what I wanted, and when I called the following Monday she told me to come at four thirty the following afternoon. I told my boss that I had an appointment and left in time to get to the Fulmer building.

The receptionist greeted me as formally as always, no hint of the real reason for my visit. Moments later she called me inside and led me down a long, paneled hallway and into a small room with a curtained wall. The receptionist turned off the lights and slowly opened the curtain so I had a great view of the room I had always met with Ellen in. The woman pulled over a high chair so I was at the right height to watch the proceedings, and left.

Within only a moment a man was shown into the room. He was balding, with a bad comb-over, florid skin, a slightly flabby middle and a flaccid penis, all of which I noticed as he undressed. With little fuss he lay on the table, facedown. Then Ellen walked in and said, "Glad to see you, Fred. How have you been?" Obviously the room was miked. I could hear everything.

Fred turned his face toward her. "Great, Ellen, but badly in need of your special services."

"I'm glad to hear that." She began as she did with me, on his back. She moved quickly to his buttocks, fingers pressing deeply into his soft flesh. From my angle I could see quite a bit, but I also became aware that one of the mirrors I'd always just taken for granted gave me a different view. My eyes flicked from watching directly to gazing into the mirror. It was almost as good as actually being in the room with them.

"Okay, Fred, turn over." He did and she massaged him. It was amazing to watch his cock grow from flaccid to erect as her fingers played over his body.

My cock was becoming erect as well so I unzipped and took it out. Then something odd happened. "Okay, knees up," Ellen said.

This was different. Fred lifted his knees until his heels were against his butt and I could see his toes wiggle. "Ready?" Ellen said.

"Of course," he said. As I watched, Ellen took a slender, plastic-wrapped dildo from a drawer beneath the sink, removed the covering and ran it beneath the water. Fred's eyes never left the instrument as she slowly dried it and coated it with oil. Oh God, I thought, feeling my cock harden still more.

She filled her palm with more oil and ran her hand over his anus. From my angle I had a direct view of his asshole, now glistening with oily moisture. She gently rubbed the toy over his skin; then I watched it slide into his ass and heard his long, low moan.

His cock stood straight out and, as she pumped the dildo in and out, she duplicated her movements on his cock until he filled her hand with semen.

I was so hot I could have come without even touching myself. I'd never tried anal penetration but it seemed so erotic that all my muscles twitched. I took a handkerchief from my pocket, wrapped it around my cock. It took only a few strokes until I came, panting.

I slowly closed the curtain, then left, eager to see Ellen again. Yes, I was ready for this next step.

# Special Services: Part Three

THE FOLLOWING FRIDAY I HAD MY REGULAR APPOINTMENT with Ellen. I quickly stripped and lay on the massage table. I knew I was becoming a massage junky, but I didn't care. I was too hot to care.

How could I ask Ellen to use that dildo on me? I didn't know whether it would arouse me as much as watching anal sex had, but I really wanted to try it. That was, as long as Ellen understood that I might want to call it off too.

She arrived, wearing her usual white blouse and dark slacks. She didn't look like a prostitute but I guess that was what she was. Labels. Hogwash. We had fun together and I paid for it. So what!

"I gather from the receptionist that you were here when Fred was last Tuesday. Did you see what went on in here?" she asked.

"Yes," I said, still feeling a little doubtful.

"Did you enjoy the show?"

Feeling a little tentative, I admitted that I did.

She said nothing more and began to work on my back. This was all a formality since my back no longer bothered me, but her ministrations did relax me and make my orgasm that much sweeter. I guess many men are impatient and want only to get their rocks off. Me, I love the anticipation.

As she worked up the backs of my thighs I imagined her fingers parting my cheeks. Moments later I didn't have to imagine anymore. She kneaded my buttocks, then pulled my cheeks wide apart, then slid her fingertips to my sac. I thought I'd come right then. I wriggled to adjust the pressure on my cock. Her fingertip then moved to my anus and rubbed around the sphincter. "Interested?" she asked softly.

I couldn't speak so I merely nodded.

Without a word she moved to the sink and washed her hands as I watched. I loved to see her move and to anticipate what she would do next.

She opened a drawer beneath the sink and withdrew a pair of latex gloves and slowly put them on. Finger by finger, hand by hand, she covered her hands in plastic. I knew exactly why and my cock twitched with expectation. "I'm not sure," I said, swallowing hard.

"First time?" Again I nodded.

"Don't worry. I know your body very well by now and you can stop me at any time, of course."

As I'd seen her do while I watched from the other room, she pulled a plastic-wrapped dildo from the drawer, tore off the wrapping and washed it. "We use new toys for each customer and you will get it to take home." No chance of disease transmission that way, I reasoned.

She oiled the dildo and her fingers, then crossed to the table. "Just relax," she said, stroking my butt and thighs. "It's going to feel *sooo* good."

She teased her way down my butt crack, a place no fingers but mine had ever been. "*Sooo* good," she purred, arousing me still more. I pressed my hips against the table to try to calm my raging hard-on.

She circled my hole with her fingertip, then with the toy. "It can be more fun if you try to keep it out," she purred. "Try hard."

I enjoyed her suggestion and clenched my ass muscles. Somehow it made it seem dirtier, as if she was doing something I didn't want rather than something I was aching for.

"You can't stop me," she crooned. "Not at all." She pressed the tip of the dildo against my ass and pushed. Thanks to all the oil it slipped in easily. I thought it would hurt, but it didn't. It felt fabulous. "See? You can't stop whatever I want to do to you."

The dildo was shaped so that once inside it didn't just slip out, but it had a wide bottom so it couldn't go any farther in either. "Maybe I'll just leave it there for you to think about." She lifted her hands from my body.

I felt filled. The plastic pressed against my prostate, an added stimulation. I thought I'd go crazy from the arousal. I was harder and hotter than I could ever remember being.

"However," she said, "I think it's time." She pulled the toy out, then pushed it in again. In and out, like she was fucking my ass. I pressed on my cock to no avail. I came, cock squeezed between my belly and the table. And I kept coming for what seemed like hours, then went limp.

She knew I'd climaxed so she slowly withdrew the toy, washed and dried it, then put it with my clothes. "No one's due in here for another half an hour so relax for a while. I'll set the timer for twenty minutes so you'll have a little time to wash and dress. Bathroom's in there." She opened the door, then paused and turned back to me. "See you next week?"

"You bet."

# The Balcony

A WARM BREEZE DRIFTED OVER MY FACE BUT I BARELY noticed. I sat on the second-floor balcony outside the hotel room my wife and I had rented on a small Caribbean island contemplating our marriage and what had gone wrong. Actually most of our relationship was wonderful. We laughed at the same things, had similar taste in movies and TV shows. Although she was a Republican and I was a Democrat we enjoyed our heated political discussions.

We'd been married almost five years, no kids by choice. We each had a high-profile job; she was a CPA and I was a lawyer. Lots of hours, lots of weekend labor, lots of money to do what we wanted in our spare time. It was all pretty good. Except our sex life sucked. I chuckled inwardly at my double entendre. Actually it didn't suck—anything. We made love perfunctorily once a week or so, sort of like scratching an itch. Our sex followed a well-established pattern, the same stroking, squeezing, holding, and the same penetration in the same position. Boring!

Elise and I had talked about it and we'd agreed to spend a week here, on this island, in a romantic setting, to try to recapture what we had. We'd arrived that afternoon, gone for a swim in the pool, had a lavish dinner with a bottle of good cabernet and gone back to the room, laughing. Then we'd made love. Sadly, we fell back into the same pattern. Same old, same old.

So as she slept I wandered out onto the little balcony and gazed at the water and the beach, wondering whether we could really put it back together.

As I sat, I heard the strains of a song I hadn't heard in several years. I remembered Elise and I dancing to it while we were dating. The moon was full and lit the area below our room brightly. A couple wandered down the beach and stopped pretty much right in front of me. They seemed to be in their midtwenties, dressed in swimsuits with bare feet. He was about my height, with a lean body and a close-cropped beard, sort of like mine. The woman had shoulder-length dark hair and a nice figure. I remembered when Elise had worn her hair long like that and how much I'd enjoyed playing with it. As I watched they turned to each other and began to sway to the music.

She dropped her beach bag on the sand and enfolded him in her arms. It was a really romantic scene, like the ones in those chick flicks my wife watched occasionally when I was involved in a case. The wind blew lightly in my direction and I thought I could smell her light perfume, sort of like the one my wife used to use. It was probably just the local flora.

There was considerable body rubbing as they danced, and I couldn't keep a smile from my face. Then he unfastened her bikini top and dropped it on the sand. I could almost feel the swell of her breasts against my chest. Very sexy. He was a lucky guy.

I saw her hands roam his back, and then their lips met in a long and hungry kiss. I sighed, remembering my wife like that. It had been so good. I assumed they'd end their erotic dance and walk on, but they surprised me by pulling a large towel from her beach bag and spreading it on the sand. They settled on it. Were they going to do it? Right there? I leaned forward and braced my hands on the railing.

His mouth found her breast and I could almost hear her long, low sigh of pleasure. He alternated between tits until she was writhing with pleasure. I felt my own cock harden as I seemed to feel what he was feeling.

Then he helped her remove the bottom part of her bikini and stretched out on the sand between her spread legs. I could almost smell the odor of her arousal and his mouth fastened on her bush. I thought I could hear her moan and the slurping sounds of his ministrations. I could see her back arch with the pleasure of it. I started to put my hand on my stiffening cock but refrained. Not yet, I told myself.

Then they shifted positions and she lay between his legs, giving one of the best blow jobs I'd ever seen. She took him deep into her mouth, then slowly drew back. If I had closed my eyes, I knew I'd be able to feel it, but I didn't want to miss anything.

Up and down her head bobbed as he tangled his hands in her hair. Again they changed position and she quickly raised herself over his cock. As I watched she slowly lowered her body onto his raging erection, her back arched, her head thrown back.

I felt a hand on my shoulder. "Remember when we used to make love like that?" my wife said.

"I certainly do," I said, watching as the couple soared toward climax. "What happened?"

"We got lazy," Elise said. "Want to try again?"

"God, yes," I said, glad I hadn't used my own hand to bring myself off. What a waste that would have been.

I stood and turned to my wife. We kissed, long and passionately. As we walked back into our room, I glanced at the couple on the sand, now replete, lying on their blanket. For a moment a cloud blocked the moonlight and when the beach reappeared, the couple was gone. Elise had seen them too and so it couldn't have been a dream or a hallucination. Could it?

## Legal Silliness

*In* HOTELS IN SIOUX FALLS, SOUTH DAKOTA, EVERY ROOM is required to have twin beds. When a couple rents a room for only one night the beds must remain a minimum of two feet apart. It's also illegal to make love on the floor between the beds! (Hmmm—in the chairs? On the dresser?)

IN VENTURA COUNTY, CALIFORNIA, CATS AND DOGS ARE not allowed to have sex without a permit. (Where do the felines and canines apply and do they sign the application with paw prints?)

A TOWN IN MONTANA HAS A LAW THAT THERE CAN BE NO sexual hanky-panky between members of opposite genders after sundown, in a front yard, if those indulging are nude. (Got that? I guess if you wear socks, do it at twilight or play on the porch, the law can't get you. And what about same-sex couples?)

CORSETS ARE BANNED IN MARYVILLE, MISSOURI, BECAUSE the law states that red-blooded men shouldn't be prevented from viewing the unencumbered body of curvaceous young women. (I hear you guys saying, "Right on!")

IN ONE TOWN IN TEXAS THERE IS A LAW AGAINST TWO PIGS having sex on the city's airport property. (Goats are okay, I guess.)

A LAW IN FAIRBANKS, ALASKA, DOES NOT ALLOW MOOSE TO have sex on city streets. (Enforce that, Governor Palin.)

IN MARYLAND, IT IS ILLEGAL TO SELL CONDOMS FROM VEND-ing machines except that: prophylactics may be dispensed from a vending machine in places where alcoholic beverages are sold for consumption on the premises.

IN HELENA, MONTANA, A WOMAN CAN'T DANCE ON A TABLE in a saloon or bar unless she has on at least three pounds, two ounces of clothing. (Okay, who weighs the clothes? And what about a G-string with lead weights on the sides?)

A LAW IN NEVADA PROHIBITS SEX WITHOUT A CONDOM (THE most sensible law I've ever read).

IN THE STATE OF WASHINGTON THERE IS A LAW AGAINST having sex with a virgin under any circumstances, including on a wedding night. (That leads to an interesting conclusion. No woman will ever be able to have a legally sanctioned first encounter unless she leaves the state.)

## International Prohibitions

*In* Lebanon, men are legally allowed to have sex with animals, but the animals must be female. Having sexual relations with a male animal is punishable by death. (Right, that makes sense.)

The penalty for masturbation in Indonesia is decapitation.

In Hong Kong, a betrayed wife is legally allowed to kill her adulterous husband, but may only do so with her bare hands! The husband's lover, on the other hand, may be killed in any manner desired. (That's right: blame the other woman—ugh.)

\* \* \*

TOPLESS SALESWOMEN ARE LEGAL IN LIVERPOOL, ENGLAND—
but only in tropical fish stores. (Huh?)

IN CALI, COLOMBIA, A WOMAN MAY ONLY HAVE SEX WITH
her husband, and the first time this happens, her mother must
be in the room to witness the act. (Aren't you glad you don't
live in Cali?)

IN SANTA CRUZ, BOLIVIA, IT IS ILLEGAL FOR A MAN TO HAVE
sex with a woman and her daughter at the same time. (Okay, I
give up. How serious must the problem have been that led to
this law?)

# Not Another Meeting!

"Not another of those meetings," Jeni's friend Tess hissed to her from the next cubicle.

Jeni was just reading her e-mail that requested—nay, demanded—her presence at a staff meeting in half an hour. "I guess it is," she said with a soft, long-suffering sigh. "Mr. Prentiss will do his usual rah-rah company, tough times ahead, let's all pull together speeches and," she said, reading further, "introduce another ad campaign guaranteed to increase sales."

"God help us," Tess said, groaning.

"And, of course, we're expected to have the latest cost analyses out by the end of the day, just as if we hadn't wasted an hour listening to Prentiss blather on."

Tess chuckled. "No rest for the weary."

Jeni spent the next half hour working on her numbers and fitting them into several complicated spreadsheets. She was good at her job and was the kind of woman who would stay late if she needed to in order to get her work done. However, she deeply resented having her time wasted. Finally, at one minute to eleven, she rose, smoothed her deep green slacks, straightened her buttercup yellow blouse and, with Tess close on her heels, headed for the large conference room.

The two women walked down the hall chatting softly. They resembled each other, both in their midtwenties, both with slender figures that they worked on at the company gym after business hours, both rather attractive but not head-turners.

Several dozen people were already present in the large room, sitting in soft leather seats around a rectangular mahogany conference table or on uncomfortable chairs situated around the perimeter. Jeni and Tess knew in advance that only vice presidents and above were permitted the luxury seats and, as anticipated, those seats were full of suits. The friends were unable to find seats near the door, so the two women settled on the far side of the room beneath the large window. "Shit," Jeni muttered. "We'll be the last ones out."

Mr. Prentiss entered, looking pompous as he always did. However, this time he was followed by a suit-and-tie-wearing, heart-stoppingly handsome guy. *Who the hell is he?* Jeni wondered, already creating a mental image of the man wearing only jeans, top button unfastened, zipper lowered, showing flat abs, a magnificent chest and great, broad shoulders. She often rearranged the facial features on the men she fantasized about, but with this hunk it wasn't necessary. He had deep brown hair, worn slightly longer than customary, flashing blue eyes and a killer smile. Stud. Hunk. Eye candy.

When she sighed, Tess jabbed her in the ribs. "Cut that out," she whispered.

Unable to deny where her mind was, Jeni hissed, "Got a better way to spend this god-awful time?"

"This is Karl Bannister," Mr. Prentiss said, "our new account executive at C and E, and he's here to fill us in on the new campaign and their cost and revenue projections for the next two quarters."

There was polite applause and the hunk stepped to the white board. "Thank you, Mr. Prentiss." His voice was slightly husky and sexy as hell. He clicked the control in his hand and the company logo flashed on the board. "As you can see . . ." he began.

Jeni drifted away. Quickly, all the people in the room faded, leaving only her and the hunk. Slowly his clothes dissolved and, as she'd pictured him when he first arrived, he was wearing jeans and nothing else. "You're Jeni," he said, his husky voice still deeper. "I wonder whether you'd be willing to do a few things for me. I'd like to work through lunch, so I could have something sent in."

"Of course, Mr. Bannister."

"Oh, if we're going to be working together, call me Karl."

"Of course, Karl."

"Good girl," the hunk said. "Come over here."

She moved from her seat by the window and crossed the room, skirting the conference table. "Yes, Karl. What can I do for you?"

In her dreams she was always a bit taller than her five foot four, and prettier, with long sable hair, deep brown eyes and, of course, great boobs and a tiny waist. In her mind she was dressed in a full, floaty skirt and tight, short-sleeved sweater, showing off her assets to perfection.

"Well, first," he said, "let's close the doors." He quickly did so, then moved to stand very close to her. She didn't back up. He crooked his index finger and used the knuckle to lift her face. "I'll bet you can imagine what services you can perform, and what I can do in return."

As an answer she merely closed her eyes. The lips that touched hers were soft and warm, brushing lightly across hers. Other than the kiss, their bodies were still. She savored the feel of his mouth as it caressed her lips, then moved along her jaw-line to her ear. The feel of his teeth on her earlobe caused a shiver to flash down her spine, and his tongue licking and prob-ing made it skitter back up again. Her knees weakened and her pussy twitched.

His lips returned to her mouth; then the tip of his tongue requested entry. She parted her lips and his tongue slipped in-side, tasting, feeling, drifting lightly over her teeth and tongue.

As she felt herself becoming limp, his hands grasped her waist and he lifted her until she slid onto the slick mahogany conference table. It was smooth and cool and felt sooo good on her heated flesh.

He made quick work of her sweater and bra, then lifted one large breast to his lips. A man's mouth on her tits always turned her to jelly and this hunk's lips and teeth were no exception. As she trembled he lifted her, moved her skirt from beneath her and lay her back on the cool wooden surface of the table. She wore no panties so her buttocks almost caressed the polished wood.

Without a word, he settled into a chair and slid her toward him until her hips were just on the edge of the table. Then his mouth was on her, lapping, sucking, licking the length of her slit.

It was heaven. His tongue flicked over her hard clit as his hands kneaded her buttocks. He held her tightly against his mouth as his tongue probed her entrance. She felt spasms of pleasure arc through her and her back arched to better join with him.

Just as she was about to climax, she felt Tess's elbow and became aware that the rest of the employees were applauding. "That fantasy of yours must have been good," Tess whispered beneath the sound of the clapping. "You were smiling and sighing. You're lucky no one else heard you."

"God, my dream was fabulous," she said, knowing that she'd have to hustle to the ladies' room and masturbate to relieve the deep itch between her legs.

People rose and slowly filed out in front of them. As she reached the door, Mr. Prentiss stopped her. "Jeni, this is Karl Bannister." They shook hands. "He's got some things he needs you for." Not waiting for any more conversation, Mr. Prentiss walked out, leaving Jeni alone with the hunk.

"So you're Jeni," Karl said. "Mr. Prentiss said you were a whiz with the projection spreadsheets. I wonder whether you'd be willing to do a few things for me. I'd like to work through lunch, so I could have something sent in."

"Anything you say, Mr. Bannister."

"If we're going to be working together, why don't you call me Karl?"

# The Maturity Ritual:
## Shara's Story

*T*HE CAVE OF DELIGHTS WAS COMPLETELY DARK. NO LIGHT penetrated from the outer cavern to this one. It was the same cave that Shara had been in ten years before for her coming-of-age ritual and that had been so amazing that she smiled when she thought of it. A wonderful man from a neighboring tribe had initiated her into the world of womanhood. For three days and nights, wonderful nights, she had stayed in this very cave with him, learning how to please and be pleased by men.

The People, her people, were very open about sexual matters and believed that all people should enjoy erotic activities. And she did. She'd been with many men, then settled down six years before with Garu. They'd been happy and she'd born three children. Now she was again in the Cave of Delights for the maturity ritual.

Every woman went through this but no one was willing to

speak of it. The coming-of-age ritual and the maturity ritual were two of the tribe's best-guarded secrets. She had no idea what to expect.

She remembered the layout of the cave from her previous visit: large, with a fire pit in the middle and several pieces of intricately decorated furniture. Why wasn't there a fire? she wondered. Did it have to be so dark?

She didn't dare move around in the blackness so she reached out and touched the cold stone of the cave wall and stood still to wait for whatever was to come. Try as she might, her eyes wouldn't adjust to the darkness, and although time passed she couldn't make out any shapes. Then she heard a whisper. "Shara," it said, sounding like it was coming from behind her left ear. "Shara, are you happy with your husband?"

"Happy? Of course."

"Think long and hard and answer again. Are you really happy with your husband? Do the two of you still have pleasures as you once did in your pallet at night?"

She hesitated. Should she tell the real truth? "We have three small children. We care for them, love them and, well, there are so many things to occupy us."

"Tell me more," the soft voice said.

"We don't have the time or a private place to do some of the things we used to do in our sleeping furs."

"Your children know what you do, and you can send them to other places. That's not the real reason. Think more."

She considered. "Garu is a fine husband." Only silence greeted her. "He's such a good man." More silence. "I love him."

"But?" the voice whispered.

She took a deep breath. "At the beginning it was an adventure to be together. But it's been so long."

"Have you forgotten the wonderful things you two used to do?"

"Oh no," she said. "I remember it all. It's just that, well, we just don't do those things anymore."

"Would you like to do them again?"

"Yes," she admitted.

"Now?"

"Right now?"

She felt a hand untie the cloth that covered her torso and let it drop to the floor at her feet. Soft fingers glided over the tip of one breast. "With me?"

She felt wetness flow between her legs. This was the maturity ritual, and whatever was done here must have been done with every well-grown woman in the tribe. It must be all right. "Yes."

"What did you most like?"

She knew she wasn't supposed to be embarrassed, but although she'd done so many things, she'd never talked about them with anyone but Garu. Even with him, they usually just did them and didn't speak of what went on. She swallowed hard. The man was behind her, and she felt one hand cup each breast and a strong, lean, naked body press against her back. She felt the hard ridge of his staff against her spine.

For a while she'd thought that the voice belonged to her husband. After all, it was whispery and faint and he could have been disguising it. But now that she could smell the manly aroma of his body, she knew this man wasn't her husband.

He played with her nipples, and his teeth nipped at the tendon between her neck and shoulder. Suddenly a third hand stroked down her belly. There were two men here?

"What do you most like?" the man behind her asked again.

"I like it all," she said, not knowing what else to say.

"This?" he asked. He bit the lobe of her ear. Just hard enough to cause shards of pain to echo through her. She couldn't suppress her shiver of pleasure. From time to time, early on, Garu had spanked her bottom during sex and she'd liked that. When was the last time . . . ?

"Ahh, yes," the voice said. "And this?" He pinched her erect nipple and hurt her. And excited her. Her knees threatened to buckle. "Umm, yes," he purred against her ear and she felt his warm breath and the vibrations of the sound through his chest. "And this?" The hand on her belly slipped down, combed through her hair, and then a finger rammed into her. She was already wet so her yelp was surprise, not pain.

"So wet," the voice of the person between her legs said. She had no idea the gender of the fingers now probing her. It didn't really matter, after all. Her knees threatened to buckle.

Then the fingers withdrew and the hand slapped her upper thigh, hard enough that she knew that if there had been light, she'd have seen red marks.

"Yes." She sighed. "All of it." Years ago she'd occasionally tell Garu that she'd been a bad girl and he'd gotten a gleam in his eye and punished her for her supposed infraction. So few times and so long ago. Why had they stopped? The children? Garu had enjoyed punishing her as much as she'd enjoyed the pain, and the pleasure that followed.

Fingers played with her labia; then a tongue lapped at her juices. "So wet," that voice said. "You must love the pain and the hot sex that follows."

The voice in her ear said, "Many women, and men too, enjoy pain and punishment. There's nothing to be embarrassed about. It makes the eventual sex so much better. Are you like that?"

She couldn't deny it any longer. "Yes," she admitted.

"This maturity ritual is so that you will remember those things you once loved." She felt herself lifted and placed, facedown, on a stone bench. The cold stone felt good against her heated skin and she sighed. She felt a soft cloth cover her eyes, then being tied at the back of her head. "This enhances all the senses," he whispered. Then she heard the sound of a fire being started in the fire pit.

She lay, contemplating what was to come, her body aroused but calming a notch as well.

Suddenly the whispery voice said, "Have you ever been restrained during punishment?" She could feel his breath against her ear and smell the masculine odor of his body, the blindfold making all her other senses more alert.

"No," she said, the idea causing another shudder to run through her. How would it feel to be unable to resist the punishment? The idea excited her still more.

"Ah, you will like that too." She was lifted from the bare stone and she heard rustling. Thick furs must have been put on the bench and she was tenderly lowered onto them, again facedown. Then hands pulled her arms away from her sides until they draped over the edges of the stone while other hands separated her legs widely. Her wrists and ankles were fastened down with soft restraints until she was unable to move, available for anything they wanted to do to her. She struggled to test the bindings and loved the restraints. Unknown partners, soft furs against her belly, the memory of the fingers in her passage, even her inability to move or see. It was all incredibly arousing.

Fingers played with her outer and inner lips; then a tongue flicked, lapping her fluids.

A slap startled her as it landed on her bottom, followed by another and another. While this was happening, the tongue kept licking. The slaps stopped and she felt something hard and smooth rub over her hot, reddened buns. A paddle? It rose and fell. It was pain, but just at the level that caused maximum pleasure.

The paddling stopped suddenly and the instrument merely caressed her heated buttocks, while a cold, thick shaft penetrated her, sliding easily deep inside her. Then fingers manipulated her clit until she could hold back no longer. She couldn't control the shout of joy as she came.

Over the next few hours she came several more times, loved by both men until she was so exhausted that she fell into a deep sleep.

THE FOLLOWING MORNING SHE WAS BACK IN HER FAMILIAR sleeping furs and as her brain slowly began to function she realized that Garu was beside her. "You look well refreshed," he said, kissing her soundly.

"I am," she said, trying not to blush as she remembered all the times she'd cried out in her pleasure.

Garu stroked down her back and seemed startled when he felt the remaining heat in her ass cheeks. "I remember when I used to do that to you," he said.

She turned over and wrapped her arms around his neck. "You still can," she said.

"There are so many things we've forgotten, and our loving has become a little predictable in the past few years. I hope we can rectify that now."

"I'm sure we can," Shara said, knowing they'd both try harder, using what she had learned about herself. She wondered what Garu had been doing while she had been in the cave. She gazed at him. No one had ever said that there was a maturity ritual for the men of the tribe, although there were rumors. All that was known was that men whose wives were in the Cave of Delights went off into the forest for a night. She saw his smile broaden as he stroked her face, and she wondered.

## The Maturity Ritual: Garu's Story

THE MEN OF THE PEOPLE HAD ALWAYS BEEN SWORN TO SE-
crecy about the maturity ritual for the males of the tribe. Everyone knew that the women entered the Cave of Delights ten years
after their initiation into the sexual ways of women but no one
ever spoke of what happened to the men.

Only minutes after Shara left, her parents arrived at their
hut. "She's not here," Garu said.

"We know that, of course," her mother said. "We're here to
take care of the children. We will bring them to our dwelling.
You can pick them up tomorrow."

Garu feigned confusion. He had hoped that there would be
something for him, a male version of the maturity ritual. "Why
would I need anyone to take care of our children?"

Shara's father laughed, a deep, rich sound. "You're leaving
for the night."

Garu smiled inwardly, not willing to show any eagerness for whatever secret rites he might endure. "Leaving?" he said with false innocence.

"Really, Garu," his father-in-law said. "You're not that stupid. Now leave us. Take the forest path toward the old temple and follow it. You'll know when you're there."

"There?"

"Just go."

Garu's in-laws had stayed with the children often so he quickly left and walked along the winding path. The temple was more than a half mile from the village so he had time to think. What would happen to him? His smile broadened. He was sure that, whatever it was, it would be delightful.

As the temple came in sight a lovely woman approached him. "Garu?" she asked.

"Yes. I'm Garu."

"Good. Come with me."

Willingly he followed the woman, enjoying the swing of her long dark hair and the sway of her generous hips. She entered the temple, a place he had seen only from the outside. Temple maidens? He had seen a few, and then only from afar, during ceremonies, but they were rumored to be the most beautiful maidens from all the surrounding villages. If the woman he followed was any indication, the rumors were true.

Finally they reached an inner chamber, the floor covered with rich woven fabrics and soft pillows stuffed with what looked like the softest down and feathers. There were several low, beautifully carved wooden benches and chairs, and tables covered with what he assumed were ceremonial objects made of gold and inlaid with gems of every color. The air was scented with incense and the room was lit by dozens of candles. From a door, partially hidden behind a wall hanging, stepped two more lovely women. All had beautiful shapes, long raven hair, reddened lips and large dark eyes. They were wearing silken fabrics shot with gold threads wound around their bodies.

"I am Amara," the one who had led him there said.

"And I'm Pella," the second one said.

"And I'm called Lista."

He remained mute, unsure of what he was supposed to do now.

Pella moved behind him and pressed her body against his back, sliding her hands around to stroke his smooth chest. "You are very handsome," she said. "I like touching you."

"I'm glad you do," Garu said, taking her wrists and kissing her palms.

"No," Amara said softly. "You're to do nothing. This is all for you."

That was fine with him, Garu thought.

Then the women began to touch and stroke him, his arms, legs, back, chest, with the softest hands he'd ever felt. Shara's were nice, of course, but roughened from the duties of being a mother. This was so sensual, nothing like his brief, barely satisfying couplings with his wife.

"No, don't think of her right now," Amara said.

Holy . . . Could she read his mind? He took a long, deep breath and emptied his brain, concentrating on the hands arousing him. His cock was growing, making a tent at the front of his loincloth. Which woman would he fuck? Or would he let them bring him off with their hands, or mouth? No matter. It would all happen as it would happen.

The stroking continued for long minutes until he was aching for relief. "I want you," he said to no particular woman.

"Not yet. You've become too used to quick, minimally satisfying unions. Now you must learn patience."

"How do any of you know what goes on with my wife?" he said, now eager for a place to release his seed.

There was no answer. He was led to a chair and he sat down, his erect cock sticking up from his lap. Quickly his wrists were tied to the arms of the chair and a band was wound around his waist, fixing him to the seat back. "Now, patience."

Hands played with his toes, others with his fingers. While he watched, Pella pinched one of her nipples until is was hard, then rubbed it against the back of his hand. He itched to turn his hand over and fill his palm with her flesh but his wrist wouldn't budge. Pella laughed softly as if she knew what he wanted to do to her.

His gaze switched to Lista on his other side. She threaded her fingers through her pubic hair and stroked her wet pussy. Then she held her wet fingers beneath his nose so he could smell the aroma of her sex. His cock twitched in the air, wetness seeping from the tip.

Then Lista lifted her knee over the arm of the chair and rubbed her wet pussy against the back of his hand. He felt how slippery she was.

While Lista pleasured herself with his skin, Amara kissed him, probing his mouth with her tongue. He wanted. God, he wanted. His body ached for release but he could get none. It seemed like hours while the three women drove his body crazy with their ministrations. At one point he thought he'd come without a touch to his cock, but they seemed to sense that and backed off a little until he came down a slight bit. But only a slight bit.

Over and over they drove him to the brink, then guided him lower.

After an eternity, the three women moved away and Amara said, "For years you've been coupling with your wife quickly and silently."

"I know," Garu said, barely able to collect his thoughts. "The children hear so much."

"So what? The People are very open about sexuality, and you can always go outside your hut or ask your parents or hers to stay with the children. You mustn't let it all go stale."

"Yes," Lista said, "that's what this ritual is all about. You must make an effort to keep Shara—and yourself—satisfied."

"It takes a little thought and some hard work to keep it fresh," Pella added. "And you need patience and the ability to wait with your pleasure until she's had hers."

"Remember the things you and Shara used to do when you first joined?"

Garu thought about their lovemaking sessions, long, slow loving, playing, teasing, even slapping her beautiful behind. He'd loved it all. Why had they stopped?

"I see you understand now," Amara said, kneeling between his knees and taking his cock in her mouth.

"You'll be with Shara tomorrow," Lista said, "but tonight is just for you."

He watched with delight as Amara's head bobbed up and down in his lap, and it took only a moment before Garu's semen filled her mouth. Climaxes were worth waiting for, he realized, as his pulses went on and on.

Several more times that night he came, each time waiting until it seemed he could last no longer. As morning light filled the temple room the women bathed and dressed him, then guided him back to the entrance. As he walked back to the village he thought of his wife. He hoped she'd had as much pleasure as he had, and they would have many more nights of enjoyment, sharing what they'd learned. He couldn't wait. He smiled to himself. Yes, he certainly could wait.

# Once a Knight

"*But* it was only a small dragon, Sire," Sir Kirk of Middlevale said. "Hardly any smoke or fire in his breath."

"Nonsense, my boy," the king boomed. "It had already burned down several houses and eaten several goats, a few sheep and one small cow. It was only a matter of time until it began on small children and graduated to beautiful maidens."

"I know, Sire, but . . ."

"No buts. You were hired to do a job and you did it. The dragon is no more and you shall have any of the lovely girls in the castle as your reward. With suitable financial considerations as well."

The financial considerations were what he'd been after, and he'd hoped that he could avoid the beautiful maiden thing. Oh, he was horny enough, but in several other kingdoms he'd taken a beautiful girl to his bed and been disappointed by her lack of reaction to his thrusting. He was very, very good with a spear, but with a cock, obviously not.

He'd done quite a bit of thinking about the issue, since it was always possible that he'd be offered such entertainment again and he wanted to be ready with a suitably noninsulting refusal. "Sire, I'm truly exhausted from my battle with the monster."

"You said yourself it was only a small dragon. I'm going to reward you no matter what you say, so choose your partner for the night."

*That tears it,* he thought. *What to do now?* He'd considered this problem too, and had come up with a possibly clever solution. He'd look around and try to find the oldest female in the room, hoping she'd not be in the mood. If she declined here or once in his bedroom, he'd be off the hook.

He looked around carefully. The girls were beautiful, arrayed in finery any woman would envy. They all simpered, preened and tried to show themselves off at their best. Blondes, brunettes, redheads, tall, short, generous of figure and slender, dozens of woman all obviously yearned to be chosen, so they could brag to their friends. Of course, who knew what they'd say about his prowess the following morning?

"Good, son, make a really considered selection. Take all the time you need and choose any woman in this room."

"Oh, Sir Kirk, pick me."

"No, me."

"No, me."

Eventually his gaze lit on an older woman seated in a corner behind an embroidery frame, working away steadily. She didn't even look up as she listened to the goings-on. Her figure, what he could see of it, was lush, her hair worn in long braids threaded with gray, her fingers graceful and nimble at her work.

"Any woman?" he asked.

"Of course. It will be a great pleasure for any of these ladies to serve you in every way."

"If you're sure, then I choose her," he said, pointing to the woman in the corner.

"You've got to be kidding," one of the beautiful blond maidens in the audience said quite loudly.

"She's older than dirt," another said.

"Maybe Sir Kirk likes boys," a third commented.

"That can't be true," yet another grumbled. "I've heard about him from other kingdoms and there's never been a mention of that."

"Felicia?" the king said, totally startled by the knight's choice. "She's been here for such a long time. There are so many younger, more beautiful women. Are you really sure?"

"I am, Sire."

"A lad, perhaps?"

Looking totally shocked, he shook his head vehemently. "No, I want her."

Totally bemused, the king nodded. "If that's what you want." He raised his voice. "Felicia!"

The woman in question looked up and glanced at Kirk. "Yes, Sire."

"You've been selected by Sir Kirk to be his partner for the evening."

She obviously hadn't been listening, so her eyes opened wide and her glance flicked from the king to the knight. "Me?"

Sir Kirk smiled his most charming smile, sure now that he'd made a good choice. She'd leave him alone and he'd be able to get a good night's sleep. He'd ask her to warm his bed in a friendly way. He did love to have a woman snuggled up beside him.

"Yes, you, Felicia," the king said loudly.

"I don't care for jokes, Sire," she said.

"This isn't a joke," Sir Kirk said. "I desire your company. I prefer real women." He wanted to add that he preferred them to empty-headed, judgmental girls but he left this thought unspoken.

"Guard," the king commanded, "show Lady Felicia and Sir Kirk to the blue suite." Still shaking his head in confusion the king added, "See you in the morning."

Bowing, he and Lady Felicia left the throne room and followed the guard to the blue suite. The room was fabulous, walls hung with expensive tapestries, furniture covered in silks and velvets, Turkish carpets on the marble floors. The guard used a taper to light several branches of candles. He was followed by several servants who carried trays of meats, bread, rare fruits and sweets of every description. Several glasses, along with a carafe of white wine and one of red, were placed on a low table. Then the entire entourage left. The last to leave was the guard who said, "Have a good evening. You won't be disturbed." As he turned to go, he added, "The bedroom is through that door and the bath beyond."

When the room was empty save the two, he settled on a low settee and she stood in front of him. "Okay, why?"

"Why what?" he said, trying to look innocent.

"Why me?"

"I like more mature women."

"Bullshit. No red-blooded knight would prefer a woman like me."

"Well, I do," he said, surprised at her low opinion of herself. She was really lovely, with a small waist and large breasts. She moved her hands as she spoke and they were as graceful as he'd seen earlier.

"Look, let's be honest here. Okay? I'm almost old enough to be your mother and I don't fall for stories like, 'I prefer older women.' Oh, wait, you said 'more mature women.' Same thing."

Sir Kirk was getting defensive, and protective of Felicia's feelings. He looked at her quizzically and she slowly deflated. "I'm sorry," she said, settling beside him and staring at her hands. "I feel like I'm being made fun of," she continued, her voice tiny. "You couldn't have wanted me for myself, so you must have had an ulterior motive for your selection. Maybe one of the others got to you and convinced you to play some kind of giant joke on me."

Kirk sighed. She looked so forlorn. "Felicia, it's not that at all."

She raised her face and gazed at him for a long moment. "I believe you. So what made you choose me?"

He sighed again. "Okay, I'll tell you the truth. I've had this happen to me several times. Slay a dragon, be rewarded with a maiden in one way or another, take her to the bedroom and . . ."

"And what? Are you unable?"

"No, no, it's not that. I'm just—well—I guess I'm not very good at it. They always go away unsatisfied and blab to the others. When I finally leave the castle everyone is whispering about me." It was his turn to look deflated.

"So you picked me hoping I wouldn't be interested in love-making."

"That's about it. And I'm so sorry to have caused you distress. We can just spend the evening together and no one need ever be the wiser."

She smiled and motioned to the table. "I've got a better idea, but I'll tell you about it later. How about we enjoy all the goodies they've left for us?"

Kirk's smile was wide and genuine. This was going to work out after all.

They spent the next hour enjoying all the food and drink, and eventually they started on the second carafe of wine. "Isn't it getting warm in here?" Felicia said.

"It is indeed," Kirk responded.

"Then let me help you with your doublet and your boots." Her hands were soft and facile as she unfastened his jacket and vest, then pulled off his boots, leaving him only in his singlet, pants and hose. "Now, that's so much better." Her voice was soft as she almost purred.

He had to admit that she was right—it was better with fewer of his heavy garments. His belly was totally full and he was a little tipsy from the wine. He draped himself across the sofa, put his feet up, and let his head fall back on the cushions. "I feel wonderful," he said, his speech slightly slurred.

"I told you I had an idea about how to spend the evening. Would you like to hear what it is?"

"Mmm," he said.

"I would love to teach you about making love."

His head flew up. "What?"

"I've been around for a long time, and I've mastered many of the arts of love. I'd like to teach you."

Shit. She wanted his body. Shit, shit, shit. How had he gotten himself into this? "I don't . . ."

Through his clothing, she put her hand on his flaccid cock and, of course, it sprang to life. "Yes, you do," she said. "And I know how to make it the best."

"Listen, Felicia, I don't think this is such a good idea."

Her smile was wide. "I do," she whispered. She leaned over and covered his lips with hers.

This was all right, he thought, enjoying the feel of her mouth. He always did like kissing but he didn't think girls did. They always seemed to be in a hurry to end it.

She moved back a hair and spoke against his mouth. "Relax. Don't be in such a rush. Let's savor each other."

*Okay,* he thought. *If you say so.* Then he jabbed his tongue between her teeth.

"Easy. Taste. Explore. Like this."

He let out a rush of air as she slowly insinuated her tongue between his lips and teeth. Her tongue played with his, then sucked at the tip. She stroked his cheeks with soft fingers and moved so her body was full length against his. "Mmm," she purred against his mouth, making a small buzzing sensation that raced from his lips to his groin. "Feel nice?" she said against his mouth.

He had to admit it did. "Yes," he whispered.

As they continued to kiss, she moved away slightly and her

hands got busy with the ties on the front of his singlet. Then her nails scraped the skin of his hairy chest until they found his flat nipples. He'd never realized they were sensitive until her fingers flicked across them. His cock responded immediately and her body undulated against him, her pubis pressed against his hardness.

"Now, do you really want to stop?" she asked, gazing into his eyes.

He moaned. "No," he said. "But . . ."

"No buts. Just enjoy."

She moved off of him and quickly removed the rest of his clothing. His hard cock stuck straight up in the air. "Just enjoy," she purred again. Then her tongue found his cock and she licked the fluid from the turgid tip. As she sucked just the head, she again moaned. "Mmm." Again the buzzing of her purr darted around his body, arousing him still further. Interesting, the small conscious part of his brain thought. He'd have to remember that.

Then he couldn't think anymore. Her mouth engulfed him and he was in ecstasy. She sucked while her tongue lapped at him. Deeper and deeper she took him into her mouth until he was totally unable to think. He was going to come and he didn't care where his cock was when he did.

And he did come, hips bucking, cock spurting, a loud groan echoing though the room.

For a long time afterward he was completely gone, dozing and waking, feeling Felicia's weight on his loins. He had no thoughts, no reason, nothing in his head. He knew it was a long time later when he finally opened his eyes and gathered Felicia to him.

"You had your pleasure, and I think it was good," she said, snuggling against his side.

"Oh, Felicia, it was." Better than he'd ever known.

"I'm very glad. Would you like to be able to give a woman as much pleasure as I just gave you?" she asked.

No. He couldn't. Yes. He wanted to learn. No. He'd disappoint her and show his lack of talent. Yes. He did want to.

"Do you trust me?" she continued.

"Yes," he admitted both to her and to himself. "But I'm afraid I'm no good at it."

"You're so silly," she said with a light giggle. "You take on dragons but you're afraid of a woman? Are you afraid of me?"

"Of course not."

"Well, I've been left without an orgasm. Oh, I loved what we did, but I haven't gotten my pleasure yet. Would you like me to teach you how to do it for me?"

He thought about it. He was both reluctant and eager. He let his eagerness win out. "If you think you can."

"I know I can."

And she showed him. All night. And all the next day.

# In Days of Old

In days of old, when knights were bold
And chastity belts were in fashion
It was elementary.
They tried some rear entry
And satisfied much of their passion.

In days of old, when knights were bold
And ladies wore no undies
Men stuck themselves out
Through the metal, no doubt
And cleaned up their armor on Sundays.

In days of old, when knights were bold
And armor was the fashion
They found a maid's cunt

Through a hole in the front
And gave in to their need for hot passion.

In days of old, when knights were bold
And ladies were prim and proper
Knights kept 'em small
No erections at all
For the codpieces were made of copper.

In days of old, when knights were bold
And rubbers weren't invented
They stuck an old sock
On top of their cock
And that is how kids were prevented.

In days of old, when knights were bold
And women weren't particular
They lined up 'em all
Against any old wall
And screwed 'em right well, perpendicular.

## About Jack and Jill

Jack and Jill went up the hill
To kiss and hug and pet.
'Twas their wedding night
And they found delight—
Well, they haven't come down the hill yet.

Jack and Jill went up the hill.
About sex they would learn.
When Jack slipped Jill his bone
She let out a loud moan.
His hearing is soon to return.

Jack and Jill went up the hill.
Jill wasn't wearing panties.
She leaned way far over

To sniff at a clover
And now all her sisters are aunties.

Jack and Jill went up the hill
Some nookie to arrange.
She took all his money
Filled her hands up with honey
And never did give him his change.

Jack and Jill went up the hill.
Each one had a quarter.
Jill's most intense,
She's got fifty cents.
Do you think they went for water?

Jack and Jill went up the hill
To drink a keg of brandy.
Jack got stewed;
Jill got screwed.
Now it's Jack 'n Jill 'n Andy.

Jack and Jill went up the hill
And planned to do some kissing.
Jack made a pass,
And grabbed her ass.
Now two of his front teeth are missing.

Jack and Jill went up the hill
For just an itty bitty.

Jill's in a state
She's four weeks late,
And Jack has left the city.

Jack and Jill went up the hill
To fetch a pail of water.
Neglectful Jill
Forgot her pill
And now they've got a daughter.

## *Show Me*

*Larry* IS SO SWEET THAT I'M AMAZED THAT NO ONE HAS tempted him into a permanent relationship yet. He's about my age, midtwenties and sort of cute. Well, not hunky, or even handsome, but he's got a gleam in his eye that says, "I'm nice, comfortable in my skin and interested in you." At least that was what his look said to me on our first date.

We met in a club, danced a little, then sat at one of the postage stamp–sized tables and talked. For hours. We agreed on some stuff and disagreed on other things. At some point I glanced at my watch and realized that it was almost one AM. "I have to be at work at nine," I said, deeply disappointed that the evening had to end.

He looked at his watch and said, "Shit. Me too. I don't want this to end."

That was only the first of many times we thought the same thing at the same time. We made a date for the following Friday and afterward we took buses home, sadly in opposite directions. We talked on the phone endlessly, dated almost every evening and quickly we were an item. We talked about sex, but didn't want to rush things. However, by our third weekend together I was more than ready.

The first time we made love it was lovely—hurried, a bit awkward, but satisfying. Larry made sure of that. I found him to be a considerate lover, always interested in my pleasure as well as his own. He climaxed that first time and when we made love for a second time he made sure I came as well. That night he stayed over for the first time.

That brings us to last evening. We were sitting on the sofa in my living room, watching a DVD. When it ended, without any preamble, he looked me right in the eye and asked, "What do you like most in bed?"

"You," I said, pretty sure that wasn't what he was really asking.

He chuckled. "No, silly. I mean what do you like most, sexually. Oral, anal, pain . . ."

I was dumbfounded. I'd read about that stuff and tried a few moderately creative things with past boyfriends, but I'd never talked about it. "I like everything," I said, hoping he'd let it drop, at least for right then. The conversation was embarrassing me.

He draped his arm around my shoulders and drew me close. He nibbled at my earlobe and whispered, "I mean it. Where do you most like to be touched? I want to learn everything about you, especially what you like in bed."

I swallowed hard. "I like everything you do." *All right,* I thought, *let it go.* I can't ask for stuff. It isn't nice.

He kissed me deeply. "I love kissing you," he said. "It gets me all hot."

*Good,* I thought. *Something I can talk about.* "I love kissing you too."

We kissed for a long time, my temperature rising every minute. Then he cupped my breast through my shirt. "I love your tits."

What can one say to that? His hands seemed to know what I liked, so why was he asking awkward questions? "I'm glad," I moaned.

"I know some of what you like too," he said. "I can read your body language, and that's really great. And I love it when you make noise. It shows that you're enjoying things."

I tangled my fingers in his curly hair and held his mouth against mine. Kissing has always been one of my favorite parts of foreplay and the electricity we create travels through me, right to my nipples and my cunt.

Larry's hands roamed my back, sides and played with my tits. He's got great hands. Eventually, when we knew that we were ready for other things, we stood and walked into the bedroom. I started to lie on the bed, but he kept me standing. He kissed a divine path down my neck and into the vee of my shirt. He hummed against my skin and it both tickled and aroused. We pulled at each other's shirttails and found naked skin beneath. His hands on me were cool; his back beneath my fingers was hot. Sensations. Fabulous.

Quickly we were naked to the waist so we kicked off our shoes and stretched out on the bedspread. He played with my breast flesh until I was writhing with the pleasure of it; then he unfastened the waist of my jeans. I lifted my hips and he slipped them off. He caressed me through the fabric of my panties. "You get so hot and wet," he purred.

Eyes closed, I moaned, showing him how much I was enjoying what he was doing.

"How do you touch yourself when you masturbate?" he asked.

My eyes flew open. "What?"

"Come on, show me. I want to become an expert on your body but you have to teach me."

He was back at it. I didn't want to talk about my most personal sex life. I wanted to make love with him.

"You can't convince me that you don't masturbate. I wouldn't believe it." He took my wrist and pulled my hand toward my crotch. "Show me where you touch yourself, where you like to be touched."

I drew my hand back and remained silent.

"Come on, baby. Don't be shy with me. If we're going to be together like this, I want to know everything."

"I want to know everything about you too," I said, my arousal level down several notches.

"Good. I was hoping you would, but I'm not too good after I come, so you first."

Had I agreed to anything? I just lay there, silent.

"Do you have a vibrator? Do you use it when you masturbate? You know, in the middle of the night when you wake up all hot and bothered."

"How did you . . . ?"

"How did I know you wake up ready to come? Lots of women do and you're such a sexy broad that I thought you might. Now, where's your vibrator?"

My eyes flashed to the drawer of the table beside my bed and, without asking, he opened it and pulled out my toy. It was battery operated and well used. He flipped the switch and the hum filled the room. He turned it off, reached out, took my hand and put the toy into it. "Show me."

"I can't." At least I was being honest for a change but I also knew my face was flaming.

"Sure you can." He took my hand, toy and all, and stroked my swollen flesh with it through my panties. "Like that?"

Actually he wasn't in the right spot. I moved my hand a little. "Good girl," he purred. "Show me."

I couldn't. Could I?

"Do you usually do it through your panties or on your naked cunt?"

I sighed long and deep. He wasn't going to let this go. I was nervous and yet very aroused by the prospect of showing him, all at the same time. It was exciting fear, like watching a monster movie through your almost-closed eyes. I gathered my courage, lifted my hips and pulled my panties off. I loved Larry but I had to admit too that we could always learn more about pleasing each other. "You said you'd show me too," I said, staving off the inevitable for another moment, "but you're wearing too many clothes."

He almost leaped off the bed, stripped in record time and lay back beside me. He leaned over and sucked my nipple. "A bonus for a very good girl. Now show me."

He reached out and turned the vibrator, still in my hand, on. It was surprisingly exciting, knowing he was watching me. I touched my outer lips and slid the vibrator down beside my cunt. I knew I was very wet and eager to touch my clit. But I delayed, as I often did.

I closed my eyes and played the toy around. I felt the bed move and knew he was leaning over, watching me. I kept my hair trimmed, so I knew he was getting a good view. It was sort of like I was performing for him. "You've got a beautiful cunt," he said.

"No one's ever said that to me before."

"Foolish other men. Watching is so wonderful. I can see how juicy you are and watch exactly where you're touching."

It was still a bit embarrassing, yet his descriptions were pushing me higher.

"I can see how erect your clitty is. Don't you want to touch it? Maybe with the fingers of your other hand?" He took my free hand and put it on my thigh.

God, I did want to touch myself. When I hesitated, he blew a hot breath of air onto my cunt, then kissed the back of my hand. I was gone. I needed so much. I put my finger beside my clit and rubbed up and down, long, slow strokes, while I played with my inner lips with the tip of the vibrator.

"Ah," he purred, "so beautiful. I love watching you pleasure yourself with both hands. Do it, baby. Make yourself come. I want to see everything." He slipped one finger into me. "I want to feel it when you come."

That did it. I climaxed then, my muscles clenching around his digit. "I can feel it, see it." He flicked his tongue over me. "Taste it. God, it's so beautiful."

When I finally dropped my hands on the bed, he took the vibrator from me, turned it off and put it aside. He kissed my neck and shoulder, then lifted one hand and sucked on my fingers. It was several minutes before I could breathe again, before the pounding of my heart slowed. When I regained my senses after one of the best orgasms of my life, I remembered his promise.

"Now you show me," I said, still breathing hard. I was intrigued. I'd seen porn stars shoot in films but I realized that I'd never seen a real man ejaculate.

He turned onto his back, his raging erection sticking straight into the air. "I won't be able to hold out long," he said.

"That's okay. Just do it so I can watch."

He ran his fingers through my sopping pussy. "For lubrication," he said with a grin in his voice. Then he wrapped one hand around his cock and cupped his balls with the other.

Did I have the courage to move so I could see better? He had. I wriggled around so I could rest my head on his thigh, gazing at his hands. I knew how the words had excited me so I said, "Show me."

He stroked the length of his cock while playing with his balls. I'd never touched a guy's balls during sex before but that was obviously giving him pleasure so I knew I would in the future.

He was right about one thing. It took only a few strokes before he spurted gism all over his belly. Once he regained his breath, he rose, cleaned up in the bathroom and brought a warm cloth to wipe my genitals.

Eventually he pulled back the covers, slid in beside me and turned off the light. He was right where he belonged, beside me, all night. Probably for a lot of nights to come.

## Amateurs Indeed

As she'd expected, Alicia found her live-in boy-friend, Dennis, in the spare bedroom playing on the computer. "What's that you're watching?" she asked.

"I found this site with film clips of ordinary people making love."

"You're watching it? Ugh, sounds boring."

"It's not, really. I've seen quite a few interesting ones."

"I'll admit that it might be amusing once or twice, but you've been in here for over an hour."

He clicked to a listing and mouse-clicked on a link to one called "Fun and Games." "Watch this."

Alicia wasn't a prude and they'd seen a few porn movies together, but amateurs? The cinematics were poor but each of the participants seemed to be enjoying the goings-on immensely. In the movies she and Dennis had watched, couples always appeared to be playing to the camera. The fact that she was watching real lovemaking, not just fucking, turned Alicia on a little.

This couple was cavorting on a thick woolly rug in front of a gas-log fireplace. She watched for several minutes as they slowly undressed each other. She had great breasts and he sucked them as he positioned her on the carpet. He was not terribly well built but he did have a large, fully erect cock.

Slowly he inserted his erection into her pussy and, even though the camera never moved, she could see the bunching of his ass muscles as he thrust into her.

Then Alicia heard heavy breathing and what seemed to be genuine sounds of pleasure, followed by a scream, hers, and a yell, his, as they came. Or at least they appeared to climax together.

"Hot, isn't it?" Dennis said. "Watching, I mean. They really seem to be having a great time."

"I have to admit that it's pretty exciting," Alicia said, unable to be coy. She found a folding chair and sat beside Dennis. "Are any others that good?"

"Sure." He returned to the menu and mouse-clicked to another clip. In this one, a woman was giving head to a guy with much slurping and noisy sucking. "I like it when you do that for me."

"I know you do," she said.

Then he clicked to a third clip. This one was quite different. Slowly, a man tied a woman to a chair, hands behind her, ankles well restrained. Alicia squirmed in her seat. "As I said, hot, isn't it?" Dennis said softly.

She was unable to speak. She'd read a few books in which someone was tied up in one of the scenes and it had always made her twitchy and sort of uncomfortably aroused. She'd been brought up to believe that it was evil to even think about those things.

As the film continued, Dennis moved behind her, grabbed her by her hair and pulled her head back. He kissed her deeply, tongue doing its magic, dueling with hers. When he stood back up, he whispered, "Tell me to stop and I will. You know that." Then he grabbed her wrists and pulled them behind her. Holding them tightly, he kissed her again.

She knew there was more passion in this second kiss and she couldn't disguise her own lust. If he said anything, she'd have to deny it, but he didn't. He left the room and returned a few moments later. She'd been unwilling to move, eyes riveted on the computer screen where the man was teasing the woman who was unable to avoid his attentions to her breasts and pubic area.

Without a word, Dennis again held her wrists and she felt soft fabric as he tied her wrists behind her. *I should tell him to stop,* she thought, but this was so exciting that she quickly realized she didn't want to. If he said one word . . . He remained silent, keeping the area between her and the screen clear so she could watch the activities.

Now he took one of her ankles and pulled it gently until her knee was beside the seat, forcing her thighs far apart. He quickly tied it to the rear leg of the chair, and followed with the other. She was wearing a light summer skirt that fell across her lap, and her panties were soaked. Dennis unfastened the buttons of her shirt and pulled it from the waistband of her skirt. Then he unhooked her bra and lifted it until her breasts were free.

Alicia's eyes glazed over, pleasure robbing her of all senses but the feeling of air on her breasts and the cool metal chair against her thighs. Then his teeth were nipping at her erect nipple. There was love but no gentleness in his ministrations. She should stop this, but it was impossible. She liked it too much.

He moved from one nipple to the other, licking, biting and blowing on her wet skin. God, she wanted her pussy filled. Now. She was so hot. But it would be impossible in this position. Well, he'd probably untie her and they'd go into the bedroom and fuck there. Sad. She'd love to see what it felt like to do it tied up like this. Shit, that's sooo bad, but I never dreamed . . .

Dennis started another video, and as he left the room she watched another guy on the screen tie the woman up. So slowly. She saw each wrist and each leg being restrained, and her juices flowed still faster.

She heard water running in the kitchen; then Dennis was back with a few things in his hands. He immediately moved behind her so she couldn't see what he had.

She found out soon enough when she heard the snick of a pair of scissors. Without a word he moved her skirt aside and she felt the cold steel against the hot skin of her hip. Snick, snick, and her panties parted. Another snick and he cut across the crotch. She lifted her hips slightly to allow him to pull the fabric away. He also moved her skirt so she felt the cold metal of the chair seat against her crotch. Her mind was unable to focus on more than the feel of her pussy.

Then Dennis was seated on the floor between her knees. "It's scrubbed," he whispered; then she saw that he was holding a cucumber. He pressed it against the inside of her thigh and she jumped. "Sorry for the cold," he said, "but that's the way it is."

Again she thought she should stop him and she knew he would if she said anything. She remained silent. She couldn't be hypocritical. They both knew she was eager for whatever happened.

Then she felt the cucumber between her inner pussy lips. "Watch," he hissed, and she looked down. The dildo slipped into her and she saw it slowly engulfed by her body. Then he leaned over and flicked his tongue against her clit. She climaxed. Hard. Long. Spasms overtook her, washed over her in waves, causing her to cry out. "Yes, yes, yes."

He quickly untied her, picked her up and carried her into the bedroom. He stripped and plunged into her waiting body. She linked her feet behind him and matched her thrusts with his.

She came for a second time when she felt the familiar tension of his climax.

They lay in silence, and dozed for a while; then she awoke to find him gazing lovingly down at her. "Lady," he said, "I didn't plan it, but I've been thinking about this for a long time."

"I never imagined. . . ."

"But now you know."

She grinned. "I certainly do."

## Snow Globe

WAYNE HAD DONE THE LOVELIEST THING. HE'D TAKEN THE cake topper with its traditional bride and groom and had it embedded in a snow globe, the two of us standing in front of a long limo. He presented it to me on our three-month-iversary and it almost brought me to tears. It was such a thoughtful thing to do. I shook it and light snow fell over the lovers. It was so romantic.

"Like it?" he asked.

I enveloped him in a bear hug. "I love it."

That evening, while Wayne watched the TV news through his toes, I gazed at the globe, now in a place of honor on my dresser. I could hear the music we'd danced to in our special spotlight dance and feel the press of Wayne's body against mine, through the three petticoats. I gazed at the couple in the glass sphere and remembered my fantasy before the wedding. I was a little sad that it had proved to be impossible.

Here's how I wanted it to go.

After the ceremony and all the picture taking, we would climb into the limo to ride to the reception hall. We'd be alone. In reality, of course, my sister and her husband had had car trouble and had ridden with us. Too bad.

I closed my eyes and pictured the way I had wanted it to play out.

Wayne handed me into the backseat of the limo and clambered in next to me, pushing the acres of my skirt aside. "I can't believe it happened. We're married."

"I know," I said, leaning against his shoulder.

He lifted my face to his. "The first kiss for Mrs. Peterson." He's a fabulous kisser and the pressure of his lips against mine aroused me. He nibbled his way to my ear and, despite my long earrings, nipped at the lobe. "I wish we didn't have to go to the reception," he said. "I want you right now."

I sighed. "I know how you feel but skipping the party is out of the question."

His long sigh was his answer. The privacy partition between us and the driver suddenly rose. I looked at Wayne. "Do you think he's telling us something?"

"I'm game," Wayne said.

"There's no way," I said.

"I think we can work out any difficulties." He reached into the low-cut bodice of my gown and scooped out one breast. His mouth found the already-erect nipple and nipped at it. I reached down and grabbed his hard cock through the fabric of his slacks.

Then he fumbled beneath the voluminous skirt of my dress and slid his hand up the inside of my thigh. When he discovered the skin above my stocking, he stroked what he's always called the softest part of me. He was driving me nuts, so I unzipped him.

One finger still rubbing the inside of my thigh, his thumb found my clit. I pulled out his cock and engulfed it in my fist. I had an old-fashioned lace handkerchief in my purse, the "something old" from the old superstition. I covered his cock with it and began to give him the best hand job I'd ever given.

He stroked my clit until I came, clenching my teeth to keep from screaming. He quickly filled the handkerchief with semen.

I came back to reality, staring at the snow globe, sighed and shook my head. Sadly it hadn't happened that way.

The news ended and Wayne saw me staring at the bride and groom. "Remember you once told me you'd fantasized about doing it in the limo on the way to the reception?" He smiled and indicated the little glass sphere. "That's why I had them put the little car in there."

Sometimes I think he reads my mind. "I do remember and I was just dreaming about it."

"I know you had the cleaner put your dress in that special box, but I was picturing you in that ridiculous fluffy dress you wore to your cousin's wedding last year."

I recalled the dress, still in the closet in the guest room.

With acres of pale blue skirt I thought I looked like an ocean liner cruising the waves. "Sure. What about it?"

"Let's rent a limo. That dress isn't your wedding dress but it's kind of the next-best thing. I could wear a suit and— Dumb idea?"

I couldn't help my grin. "I think it's a fabulous idea." Wayne is the best!

*Heat*

CAROL AND JAKE MOVED INTO THEIR NEW HOUSE WITH
the usual fears of new homeowners. However, they both worked
long hours and earned salaries large enough to be able to comfortably afford the small mortgage they'd taken out. Over the first
few weeks they explored their new digs, delving into closets, pok-
ing around in the attic and making love in each of the bedrooms.

"What's this dial for?" Jake called from the bathroom one
Saturday morning.

"Which dial?" Carol said from the bedroom.

"Come in here and I'll show you." Carol, still in her robe,
entered the bathroom and saw the wall dial Jake was pointing
to. "This one."

"I've no idea. I never really focused on it."

"Well, as long as it's not the self-destruct," he said with a
laugh as he twisted it.

A bright orange lamp in the ceiling went on. "That's wonderful. It's a heat lamp for drying your body," Carol said, obviously delighted.

Since Jake was still damp from his shower, he dropped his towel and stood beneath the light, soaking up the warmth. "You're right. This is great," he said. "It feels as good as sunshine, but without the dangers of skin cancer." He extended his arms and reveled in the warmth.

"I think little Willie enjoys the feel too," Carol said, staring at Jake's growing erection.

Jake looked down. "It's a very sexy feeling," he said. "I'll show you." He untied the sash on his wife's robe and slipped it off her shoulders. He quickly pulled her nightgown off as well.

Jake watched his wife's nipples swell. "Now, doesn't that feel great on the boobs?"

"It really does. You know I've always wanted to go to a nude beach. This feels like I've imagined being naked in the sunshine would feel."

"You're right. Okay, let's get the full effect," Jake said. "Lie down."

Carol snorted. "Don't be silly."

"Why not?" He bent down and patted the bath mat. "It's soft. Stretch out, close your eyes and we can pretend."

"It's a little small to be comfortable."

Jake opened the bathroom door just a bit so they could stick their feet out through the doorway. Then he settled on the rug. "Come on. It's the next-best thing to a nude beach."

Slowly Carol stretched out and extended her arms above her head. "I have to admit that you're right. This feels wonderful."

"Heat on parts of you that have never been exposed to the sun before. It's got Willie thinking really kinky thoughts."

Carol reached over and put one hand on his now fully erect cock. "I can tell that."

"Okay, now close your eyes and imagine the sound of the surf."

They lay for a few moments with Carol's hand resting on Jake's cock. Then Jake's hand found Carol's breast, circling her hard nipple with the tips of his fingers. He could hear Carol's breathing thicken.

"I've got an idea," Jake said. "Raise your knees."

"Why?"

"Trust me," he said with an exaggerated wolfish growl. "Just trust me." When Carol lifted her knees, Jake said, "Now spread them."

When Carol took a breath to speak, Jake said again, "Trust me."

Carol did what her husband asked. "Keep your eyes closed and feel the heat on your pussy," he purred in her ear.

"Damn," she said, "that's wonderful."

"I thought it might be. That's why my Willie is getting so hungry for you."

He propped himself up on one elbow and looked from his wife's face to her pussy. He could easily see that her juices were flowing. "Feels fabulous, doesn't it?" Then his fingers found her, combing through her pubic hair to her hard clit. He used some of her wetness to lubricate her skin and rubbed her clit in just the way he knew she liked it.

He watched Carol tilt her pelvis so his fingers and the heat of the lamp could act on her vaginal tissues. He bent over and took one erect nipple in his mouth and sucked on it hard. "Shit, Jake," she said. "You're getting me really high."

"Good," he said. "I don't want to be the only horny one around here."

Carol grasped his cock and squeezed, her thumb rubbing the fluids leaking from the tip around the head.

Jake could wait no longer. He rolled onto his wife and plunged his erect shaft into her sopping body. It took only a few thrusts for him to arch his back and yell out his climax.

As he rolled back off Carol's body, she said, "You came so fast."

"No problem, love." He crawled to a position between her legs and flicked his tongue over her flesh, wet with the combination of his and her fluids. "You taste of me," he said, licking the length of her slit with the flat of his tongue.

"Oh, God, do that. It feels soooo good."

He continued licking, then slipped one finger into her channel. "Yes," she cried. "Like that." He fucked her with his finger and leaned back so that the heat lamp could warm the skin of her inner thighs and pussy. Almost immediately he felt the familiar clutching as her muscles spasmed around his finger. Her hips bucked as she came with a long, low moan.

Later they limped to the bed and collapsed. "That was amazing," Carol said.

"Yeah. You know we should really consider taking a vacation to somewhere with a nude beach."

"Why? We have one right here."

# What We're Really Saying

- The word *penis* is from a Latin word meaning *tail* while *vagina* is from the Latin meaning *sheath* or *scabbard*. The word *vanilla* is of similar origins, so called because of the shape of its pods. Ice cream, anyone?

- Many of the slang terms for *penis*—*wang*, *dong*, etc.—arose from the fact that the word *penis* was not to be uttered in polite (or not so polite) company.

- The word *schlong* is from the Yiddish word for snake.

- The assumed derivation of the word *fuck*, that its meaning derives from "For Unlawful Carnal Knowledge," is an urban legend. The word is ancient but since it was among those that were unprintable, the true origins are unknown.

- The word *fornication* actually comes from the Latin word for *arch*. It is said that in ancient Rome, street prostitutes hung around the arches outside the Colosseum, waiting for men who were sexually aroused by the bloody goings-on within.

- The word *masturbation* comes from the Latin meaning *to pollute yourself*. Make of that what you will.

- The term *scumbag* actually refers to a used condom.

- The name for Wyoming's Grand Teton mountains means, literally, the Big Tit mountains.

- *Gymnasium* actually comes from the Greek meaning *to exercise naked*. Take that, Gold's Gym.

- Last but certainly not least, the word *pornography* comes from the Greek word for *prostitute* while *erotica* comes from Eros, the Greek god of love. So there!

# The Eroticist

*EROTICIST.* I MADE THE WORD UP, OF COURSE. I FIGURED that if a philatelist collects stamps and a numismatist collects coins, an eroticist must collect sex toys. Okay, maybe not, but I'll use the word here anyway.

I love to prowl the "adult toys" sites on the Web and, since there are still some that send paper catalogs, and since I buy lots of stuff, I'm on every list possible, both snail and e-mail. Many of the things I buy are real rip-offs, but every now and then I find something dynamite. And, of course, since I often look at items with my wife, Amy, everything an eroticist does results in great sex. I've been thinking of spreading the word and maybe this tale is the way to do that.

Let's take a few examples. One evening recently Amy dragged a chair up beside me as I surfed the net. New sites pop up with amazing frequency so I was checking out recent additions and adding the ones that showed promise to my favorites list. "Find anything good?" she asked.

"Sure," I said, clicking over to a site with lots of unusual toys. "How about these?"

Displayed on the screen were a selection of the most beautiful long, slender dildos in varied colors, with patterns and designs painted around the shafts. "They're made of glass," she said, reading the descriptions. "It says it's some kind of special glass that's super tough and resists chipping and cracking. 'You can experiment with cold or warm sensations by placing it in ice or in hot water,' it says." She wiggled her fanny. "Sounds really hot."

"Or cold," I added with a chuckle. "Shall we get one?"

Together we selected a "four ways to pleasure" blue-and-white-striped one and I clicked on "Place Order." The merchant took PayPal and I paid extra for expedited shipping. "The eroticist strikes again," I said with a cackle.

Several days later a large box was sitting on the porch when I arrived home from work. It had a well-disguised return address, but I knew what it had to be. As I usually do, I put the still-closed box on the sofa—thank heaven we live by ourselves—and waited for Amy to get home. We agreed to wait until after dinner, but I know that we both wolfed down our chicken and noodles.

We stacked the dishes, then adjourned to the living room and our package. I let Amy do the honors and, after she waded through all the catalogs and other promotional material, she withdrew a beautifully wrapped box. Inside was the dildo. It was really a work of art with a shaft about one inch in diameter and odd shapes at either end. She found a slick paper manual but I snatched it out of her hand. "Go take a shower and I'll figure out how to get the most out of this little beauty."

Leaving the toy in my hands, she disappeared into the bedroom. I read the instructions, washed the toy, then filled insulated cups, one with water and ice cubes, one with water just above body temperature.

When I finally entered the bedroom, Amy was lying on the bed, wrapped in only a towel. "Ah, I see you're ready to play," I said. "Okay, let's see how this feels."

Since we'd had no foreplay, she was in the mood but not terribly aroused. Yet.

I put the cups on the bedside table and sat next to her hips. I stroked her belly with the toy. "Feel nice?"

"Yeah," she said. "It's really smooth and sort of slippery."

I pulled her towel open and rubbed it over her breasts. Her nipples hardened quickly and, as I brushed the toy across first one, then the other, they tightened further. "Open your mouth," I said and she complied. I caressed her lips with it, then pushed the glass phallus inside, watching her give it a great blow job while I fucked her mouth with it.

I withdrew it, stroked it over her torso, then slowly rubbed it through the folds of her now-slippery pussy. "Ready?" I asked.

"Oh yes," she said, then thrust her hips upward as I slid the dildo inside. The long end was slightly curved so I used it to find all the particularly delicious places along her channel. Then I pulled it out and, while I leaned over to lick her inner lips, I put it in the cup with the icy water. "That feels great, what you're doing," Amy said, panting.

"Umm," I said against her slit and I knew the vibrations of my lips would urge her higher. I wanted her really hot. Then I reached for the chilled dildo and quickly thrust it inside her, keeping my hot mouth on her clit. "Shit," she said with a gasp.

But she came. Right then. From the combination of the cold toy and my hot mouth. I love playing with sensations.

As she slowly came down, I put the toy in the warm water. There was a thickened area toward the other end so, when the toy was warm, I turned it around, pushed it inside and rubbed her passage with the thickened bulge. It took only a few thrusts for her to come again.

"Baby!" she cried.

"Oh, yes," I said, stripping as quickly as I could and ramming my cock into her. I was so hungry from watching her come that I climaxed almost immediately.

Score another one for the eroticist.

## More from the Eroticist

〜✦〜

I PROMISED THAT I'D TELL YOU A FEW TALES, SO HERE'S another.

One evening last month I shopped alone. As she is every Tuesday evening, my wife, Amy, was out with a few of her girl-friends so I thought I'd find a little present for her. I did indeed, and I decided to have this order delivered to my office so I could surprise her the following week.

The following Tuesday she got home about ten, and, as she usually does, she walked into our bedroom and dropped her coat on the chair. "Hi, darling," she said, leaning over to peck my cheek. "Have a good day?"

"You're late," I said with a wink, "and I know that you've been out carousing with your friends. Pick up any cute guys?"

Amy catches on very quickly. She knew I wasn't really accusing her of anything and I certainly don't mind that she spends time with her friends. It was all a setup for what was to come, and her wink back told me that she was as eager for fun and games as I was. "I didn't do anything," she said, a slight whine in her voice.

"I'll just bet," I said. "Well, I've got a few things to help you remember what you can and can't do for next time."

She dropped her gaze but I caught the beginnings of a grin.

She was wearing a lightweight blue sweater, and I pointed to it. "Get it out of my way," I ordered, and she quickly lifted it. I had my first toy in my hand so I pulled one bra cup aside and fastened a suction cup on her soft bud. I'd already tried it out on my body to be sure it wouldn't be too tight, so I knew that it would be stimulating without causing too much discomfort.

I flipped the bra cup back in place, repeated my actions on her other breast and pulled her sweater back down. Now I could see the bulge at the point of her breasts. "How does that feel?" I asked.

"It's strange," she said. "It's like constant, very soft sucking." She wiggled her shoulders. "Makes me hungry."

"Good, because I've got another present for you. Panties off," I said.

She was wearing a skirt, so she bent down and removed her panties, leaving her thigh-high stockings and heels in place.

"Put this on," I said, holding out a strange-looking contraption. It appeared to be a pair of tight latex pants, with two dildos fixed in place, one for the front and one in the back. We'd enjoyed anal sex before, so I knew she wouldn't object to that aspect of it. But both? With one toy?

She looked at me, then at the pants. I'd put a tube of lubricant in my pocket, so I used some to make both dildos slippery.

Then I helped her pull the pants up and insert the toys in each of her holes. I saw her knees quiver and she almost lost her balance as both her holes were filled.

"I want a burger," I said. "Let's go to the drive-through."

"Like this?" she said, horrified.

"Just like that." I helped her on with her coat and took her arm. We walked, Amy a bit unsteadily, to the garage and I assisted her into the passenger seat. "Pull your skirt aside so I can see the pants," I said and she did. Lord, she looked so hot, the tight latex against her skin, the slight bulges on her breasts. Nothing would be obvious to anyone outside the car, but I knew how the suction cups were playing with her tits and the dildos filled her openings.

I drove to the drive-in, deliberately picking roads that were a little bumpy. One of the housing complexes in our area has just put in speed bumps and I purposefully bounced pretty hard over them. With each jar, she gasped. "Feeling good?"

"Damn, yes," she panted.

At the drive-in window I ordered a burger and a soda, then asked, "Want anything?"

"Not anything they can give me," she said with a wide smile.

I got my food, then maneuvered into a parking space by the restaurant to eat. "Why don't you eat at home?" she whined.

"I'm happy here."

"I'm not."

"Good," I said, taking a large bite.

Finally I could stall no longer and we drove back home, over the speed bumps of course. She couldn't control her cries of pleasure.

At home I told her to strip but leave the toys in place. I also removed my clothes. I unfastened one suction cup and flicked my tongue over her erect nipple. She went crazy, trying to fuck the two dildos still filling her. I understood that, since they were immobile, they weren't giving her the kind of stimulation she wanted.

I reached into my pocket and flipped two switches on a small box. "Another little surprise," I said, and I knew from her expression that the directions had been accurate. The two dildos had begun to vibrate. She screamed and came. What a great toy, I thought.

I pointed to my thick, erect cock and she quickly got onto her knees and took my member into her hot mouth. Then she got up and rummaged in our toy drawer. She drew out a cock ring and fastened it around my erection, balls and all. It would keep me from coming until she was good and ready to let me.

Then she gave me the best blow job ever. She sucked and licked, kissed and licked until I was half crazed. "Want another burger?" she asked with a gleam in her eye.

"Not likely. Now take that thing off me."

"Please?"

"Oh, baby, I'll beg if that's what it takes. Please, please, please!"

She unhooked the cock ring and almost immediately semen boiled from my balls, coating her face. I collapsed onto the bed.

Tomorrow I'll surf more sites and see what I can treat us to. I love my job as eroticist. It's a tough job but I can do it.

## The Kids Are Gone

"THE KIDS ARE GONE," MY HUSBAND, FRANK, SAID WITH A long sigh as we pulled our car into the garage. "All of them."

We had just driven our older daughter back to her college for her sophomore year, followed by our younger to hers for her freshman year. Both would easily settle in and we were confident that they'd be happy with their courses. We'd met their new roommates and thought that, in both cases, the matches were good ones. Now we were home, in an empty house.

Our two older sons were both married and lived within a hundred miles of our place. They visited from time to time, but they were both involved in their own lives, wives and children. We were alone in our four-bedroom house for the first time in almost thirty years.

"Let's rent out their rooms so no one can come back," my husband said with a chuckle.

"I'm for that."

"Actually I had a better idea," Frank said as he closed the garage door behind the car and got out of the driver's seat. "I saw an article on the net about a couple who turned their guest room into an erotic playground. Nothing that couldn't be quickly camouflaged in case of visitors, but a playroom nonetheless."

I climbed out and raised a doubtful eyebrow. "Do you think we could do it so that we wouldn't be found out?"

"I'd love to try," Frank said with a leer and a pinch at my bottom.

A small smile crept onto my face. "Me too."

Frank and I had always had a creative sex life, at least to the extent that we could with a house full of kids. In the early days we wandered into anal sex, a little spanking, and lots of toys of all sorts that were even now hidden in the back of our bedroom closet. We'd talked about bondage games but we quickly discovered that, unless we made a reservation at a motel, which I will admit we'd done from time to time, we didn't have enough privacy. Now we had all the secrecy we wanted.

Over the next few weeks we read and shared several articles, letters and Web site addresses. "It's definitely possible," Frank said one evening, "and it wouldn't even cost much."

"From what I've read we can do most of the work ourselves."

"And much of the *furniture* can be disguised as just furniture."

We drew up plans and began. We gutted TJ's old room, because it had a sloping roof beneath which we could install hidden, lockable cabinets. We installed hooks in the ceiling and hung large planters on them, pots that could be easily removed when we needed. We hung heavy but nice-looking drapes so we could isolate the room from any prying eyes.

We bought what could be described to friends and family as a massage table and I told a few people that I was thinking of taking classes. Everyone we told thought it was a fine idea.

Frank is pretty handy with tools and has a small woodshop in the basement. There he built a few essentials for playing with bondage, while I used my sewing talent to make soft, fur-lined cuffs and straps.

Fortunately we have a very large dog so buying choker collars, chain leashes and leather harnesses was pretty easy.

While this was going on, our sex life had never been better. We fucked several times a week. I could call it *lovemaking* and in one sense it was, but our couplings were so frantic and hot that it was really best termed *fucking*.

As a final step, we camouflaged the room by moving my sewing table into one corner and setting up a leather crafting area for Frank.

We'd decided to christen the room on a Friday evening. We'd talked about role-playing and which one of us would be dominant. Or course those discussions always led to hot sex. Neither of us had a strong preference, although I did admit that being submissive felt better to me. That afternoon Frank and I both came home from work early, ate a quick meal and walked upstairs into our playroom.

"I want to play," Frank said, "but I'm not sure how to begin. Can I just say take off your clothes? Does that seem too abrupt?"

I smiled. "It gets the message across." I slowly removed my clothing, teasing him a little by folding my garments carefully and putting them on my sewing chair. We've seen each other naked thousands of times, but this time was going to be special. To that end I'd bought a little body jewelry, a chain that hung around my waist with a section that slipped from the middle of the front, back between my legs, and fastened just above my butt. I'd slipped it on before dinner and it had been increasing my erotic tension ever since.

"Mmm," Frank purred. "Something sexy has been added. How strong is that chain?"

"It's slender but the ad said it was 'steel strong.' Wanna check?"

He yanked on the chain to draw me toward him. The links held easily. He grabbed the back of my hair and yanked my head back as his mouth found my throat. His teeth grazed my skin as he bit his way up the side of my neck. He pulled up on the chain and the one between my legs bit lightly between my inner lips. "Not too hard," I whispered and he lessened the pressure. "Mm, like that," I said, enjoying the feeling of possession.

We kissed and hugged; then I scratched the back of Frank's neck and pulled his hair. He moved away. "Enough of that. Over here," he said, crooking his finger. "I've made a few things and bought others. Let's see how we can make this work best."

He removed one of the plants and set it in a corner, then guided me beneath the now-revealed hook. He'd built in a mechanism that could raise and lower the hook and was adjusted with a chain on one wall. To everyone else it would look like a decorated swag for a hanging lamp or for watering plants. We knew better. "Arms," he said.

While he fetched something from our concealed closet I extended my hands. He emerged with a pair of padded handcuffs. "Let's try these," he said, snapping them on my wrists. He clipped a length of heavy chain to the area between the cuffs and lowered the hook. He fastened the chain to it and raised the level until I had to stand tall, my arms stretched above my head.

It felt awkward, but highly erotic, to stand, fastened to the ceiling, for whatever my husband had in mind. The insides of my thighs were wet and my body quivered with excitement.

Frank gazed at me, licking his lips. He was quite obviously getting as much erotic pleasure out of this as I was. "Yes," he whispered. "Just as beautiful as I knew it would be."

He pulled a length of wood about eighteen inches long from the closet and placed it on the floor behind my feet. I could see that there were lengths of Velcro attached to each end. "Spread your legs."

We discovered that he had to lower the hook a little to enable me to keep my balance, but in short order he had fastened my ankles to the ends of the spreader bar so that I couldn't close my legs. It was a heady feeling, total helplessness, my arms above my head, my legs widely parted. He had access to all of my body and it made me nuts. I wanted him to fuck me right away—I didn't even consider how—but Frank had other plans.

"Hot, baby?" he asked.

I slowed my breathing. "Hell, yes. I think I could come without much more stimulation."

"Better calm you down a little." He fetched a dildo from the closet and, moving the chain between my legs to one side, stuffed it into me. When moved back into place, the slender chain held it inside me. Then he kissed me and squeezed my ass. I was gone. My entire body shook with the force of my climax and it lasted for what seemed like hours.

When I was calmer, Frank said, "That should take the edge off."

He rolled a kneeling chair between my legs and when he was comfortably settled his mouth was at just the right height to play with my clit. His tongue roamed my slit and, although I wanted to clamp his head between my thighs, the spreader bar wouldn't allow it. I could do little but enjoy the sensations he was bringing to my body.

After my second orgasm, I said, "My hands are beginning to fall asleep," and he quickly and solicitously unfastened me. As I clenched and unclenched my fists I suggested that he remove his clothing and see how it felt.

He complied, and I hooked him to the ceiling as I had been. He looked as hot as I had been, his face flushed, his breathing hard and fast. I fastened his ankles to the wooden slat and watched as his hard cock bobbed in the air. I knelt on the kneeling seat and, as I had expected, his cock found my mouth.

I love giving my husband a good blow job and I took my time. I sucked the length of him into my mouth, then created a vacuum and pulled back, watching his erection slowly revealed as it emerged. Again and again I sucked it in, then let it out, flicking the tip of my tongue over the tip of him, tasting his tangy precome. I cupped his buttocks and forced his cheeks apart, slipping my finger between and rimming his ass.

With a loud roar, he filled my mouth with his come and, although I tried, I couldn't quite swallow it all.

Later, entwined in bed, we talked about how aroused the evening had made each of us. "I don't know which I enjoyed more," I admitted, "dominant or submissive."

"Me neither. I guess we'll just have to keep trying and see what settles in."

"Lord, how I love experimentation. And I've got several more delicious ideas."

"Me too," Frank said, sleepily.

I can't wait.

# A Three-Step Program

⁘

My husband, Ben, and I have been together for almost two years and we have an unusual method of sexual communication. We both read a lot and sometimes we enjoy erotic short stories. Several months ago we began to leave each other messages on notes in the storybooks. "Hey, babe, read this story. It really got to me." Or "Ben, baby, wanna try this?" We don't read the story when the other is around and we're obviously free to just ignore the whole thing. We don't often do that, although once I did suggest a little light bondage and Ben told me later that he wasn't into it right then. We always leave the door open for the future, however.

It was amazing that we could message about things we didn't want to talk about right out, face-to-face. A few weeks ago Ben left a bookmark in a scene in a novel where the guy has anal sex with the woman. Since I read the scene when Ben wasn't around, I found myself relaxing and not giving in to the knee-jerk "not interested." I thought about it and didn't know how I felt. It sounded painful, but lots of people do it so there must be something there.

I went to the Web and read, printing some stuff out for Ben. There was one site that suggested a three-step program to see whether the partner found it exciting. I gave the article to Ben with a bookmark.

The next time we made love he used his hands and mouth to work me up into a lather, then used my juices to lube my ass. Then he just rubbed his finger around the opening, being careful not to spread any material forward, toward my pussy. I was surprised to realize that the feel of his finger around my anus made me hotter. "God," I said, "that feels really good." We try to let each other know what's working and what's not.

His cock was hard—I guess thinking about fucking my ass sometime in the future—so he rammed it into my cunt and came in only a few strokes. I astonished myself by coming just as quickly as he did. We collapsed afterward and softly Ben whispered, "I guess step one was a success."

Still breathless, I said, "I guess so."

We'd had sex once since the rimming incident and it had been delicious. However, I found myself a little disappointed that he didn't attempt to continue our journey. I worried that he'd given up for some reason, or that he hadn't enjoyed it, but I needn't have had any doubts.

A package arrived in the mail about a week later addressed to Ben and I gave it to him when he arrived home from work.

"I know what's inside," he said, "so I suggest that we wait until later to open it."

Occasionally Ben will buy a toy for us and then tease me by not letting me see it until bedtime, so I tried to remain patient.

After we stuffed the dishwasher Ben guided me to the bedroom, sat me on the side of the bed and put the package in my lap. I tore off the brown-paper wrapping and pulled open the box. Inside was a long, slender dildo with a wide flange at the end, and a tube of lubricant. "If you're up for this . . ." he said, knowing I understood what he was asking.

"We can always say stop if it gets too much, and I must admit that I'm intrigued."

Ben washed the dildo and put it and the lube on the bedside table. Then we kissed. My lips tingled with the familiar feel of him and when they parted, his warm supple tongue gently probed inside. He tasted hungry and hot, telling me with his motions how aroused he was.

He sucked and licked his way down my neck while his large, talented hands wandered over my body, exciting and heating me. Slowly he removed my clothing, making love to each part of my body as it was revealed. When he pulled off my panties he played in my crotch, stroking and nibbling my flesh, but not touching my clit. I squirmed, trying to get his fingers or his mouth where I wanted them, but to no avail. His teasing was relentless.

Finally, when it seemed like I had been waiting for hours, he reached for the dildo. We both knew that the lube would probably not be needed. My juices were flowing freely.

He played in my pussy with the toy until he thought I was ready, then slid it back toward my anus. He rubbed the tip around my puckered hole; then we came to the moment of truth. Gently he inserted the end of the thin phallus into the sphincter and pushed softly. "Sweetheart?" he whispered.

Incapable of speech at that moment, I merely nodded. He slipped it inside. It drove me crazy. There was no pain, just a slight feeling of fullness, and shards of pleasure went right to my vagina. I came. My tremors were so violent and so sudden that they took my breath away. Leaving the dildo in place, Ben drove into me and grunted his orgasm. Later he whispered, "Step two."

We played that way a few times after that, and we eventually used a thicker dildo that we had in our toy collection. Feeling filled was fabulous. I was becoming addicted.

Finally Ben decided it was time to use his hard cock in my rear. Once I was aroused and ready, he put on a lubricated condom. We had agreed that although we'd been together for a long time, it was a good idea for health and ease of penetration.

We played with the dildo and then Ben spread lots of lube around my anal opening. It was cool and, rather than calming me down, the cold raised my sexual temperature. I thought he'd do it doggie style, but he curled me on my side and cuddled his body against my back. I felt his cock probing between my cheeks until it found my hole. He pressed forward slowly and I arched my back to give him better access.

Gently he pushed, and his cock penetrated easily. It took my breath away and I breathed, "Wait. Just like that."

He started to pull back but I reached around and grasped

his rear cheek, holding him still. I was more filled than I had been with the toys, but I was surprised that it didn't hurt. After a minute to get used to the feeling I pressed back, lodging his cock more deeply inside.

Ben let me set the pace and I thrust my ass backward, then relaxed, sliding his cock in and out. "Yes, baby," I said and released his ass. He understood and slowly increased the pace until he was fucking my ass. He reached around and found my clit. He rubbed it until I came, then let himself come as well.

Afterward we showered together. Grinning beneath the spray, he said, "Step three. Bravo!"

# *More Sexual Trivia*

- While the largest percentage of men have erect penises about six inches long, there's such a wide variation that this measurement encompasses less than 24 percent of men.

- The smallest erect penis was one centimeter long, while the longest is supposedly just over twelve inches. I can't help but wonder what woman has a vaginal canal long enough to accommodate all that.

> There once was a young man from Kent
> Whose thing was so long that it bent.
> To avoid any trouble
> He put it in double
> And instead of coming, he went.

But I digress.

- It is said that the penises of some Kalahari Desert bushmen are semierect at all times.

- According to several surveys, 97 percent of men say they masturbate. Personally, I think the rest are lying.

- The Kinsey Report states that 50 percent of men raised on a farm say they've had sex with an animal.

- The two leading causes of temporary impotence are tight pants and prolonged cigarette smoking.

- The initial spurt of ejaculate travels at about twenty-eight miles per hour. The world record for the hundred-yard dash is just under that.

- About .3% of men can actually give themselves a blow job.

- Semen contains about five calories per ejaculation, and has small amounts of more than thirty elements, including ascorbic acid, fructose, cholesterol, citric acid, lactic acid, nitrogen and vitamin B12.

- The first condoms were invented in the late 1800s. They were made of rubber, obviously annoyingly thick and meant to be reused. *Viva* the twenty-first century!!

- In Japan, the leading country for condom use, they are sold door to door by women.

- Take care, guys. That condom you carry in your wallet is probably no good anymore. A condom loses its protective ability after about a month near the heat of your body.

- Only about 40 percent of women say they enjoyed sex the first time, while 84 percent of men did. Surprise, surprise.

- Rumor has it that one in four Britons will have sex in the parking lot after the annual holiday party.

- Australian women are most likely to have sex on the first date.

# My Bound Lover

THEY SAY THAT SOMETIMES, IN A MOMENT OF SEVERE DIS-
tress, your life flashes before your eyes in a split second. Well, in
a moment of sexual excitement, a fantasy of mine flashed before
my eyes in a split second.

Before I get to the details, let me tell you a little about myself. I'm in my late twenties and rather shapely if I do say so
myself. I'm a data-entry specialist at a large insurance firm and
spend many a boring day inputting numbers into a program
designed to—well, I've really got no idea where the data goes
when I'm done with it. The work is tedious, but it pays my bills,
gives me health insurance and leaves me time for myself on the
weekends.

My fantasy began while I was surfing the Web for erotic
stories, something I do from time to time when I'm bored or
between boyfriends. I found a site with bondage stories and

photos and got so caught up in reading that I actually lost track of time. At one in the morning I finally regained control of my mouse, shut down my computer and went to bed. Hot. Horny. Fully aroused.

I'd masturbated twice during the evening to relieve the tension but I was still excited. I closed my eyes and pictured the guy of my dreams. Hunky, smooth, muscular, a real stud. He's tied to my bed, naked. Big sigh. His arms are stretched above his head with his wrists securely fastened to the headboard. His widely spread ankles are tied to the sides of the footboard and he is blindfolded. He's mine to do with as I please.

Bigger sigh. As I picture him my hand goes to my breasts and I begin to play with my hard nipples. This masturbation would be different from the ones during my reading. Now I had time to revel in all the sensations while I played with the images in my mind.

My hunky guy is fully erect, his cock long and thick, twitching as he wonders what will happen next. "You want it, don't you?" I say, watching his cock react.

"God, yes," he answers. I run my fingernail down the length of his erection and watch a small drop of precome form at the tip.

"Maybe, when I'm ready. That okay with you?"

He smiles. "What choice do I have?"

"None," I say, smiling. He can't see my smile, of course, so he's got no idea what I'm thinking.

I climb onto the bed and straddle his waist, rubbing my sopping pussy against his belly. Then I lean over and rub one nipple against his lips. Immediately he opens his mouth but I tease both him and myself for a while, then let him suckle.

Shards of pleasure stab through me, from nipple to pussy, and, in my own bed, my hands pull and twist, imagining the feel of his lips and teeth. "Suck harder," I tell my bound lover and he does, increasing my erotic pleasure.

I replace one nipple with the other and order him to suck. He does, and it's wonderful. I'm flying. In my fantasy, with the small part of my brain still functioning, I wonder how I want to come. I can make him use his mouth to pleasure me, or his cock. Maybe both.

I pull back and turn so my bush reaches his mouth. "Lick slowly," I say. I love to have my slit gently stroked by a talented tongue. He presses too hard so I teach him. "Lick the length of my slit very slowly and gently. Don't rush."

He learns. "Flick my clit," I tell him, "then use the flat of your tongue to stroke it lightly."

He's learning very quickly. "Now make your tongue pointed and push into me. Fuck me with your tongue." I sigh. "Yes. Like that."

Then he says something that almost pushes me over the edge. "Am I pleasing you?" He doesn't say "mistress," but the feeling is there nonetheless. I love that.

In my bed my hand travels down my belly toward my snatch. It's difficult to wait to relieve myself, but I want to make it last.

He's learning exactly how I like to be licked and it's becoming more and more difficult to resist his cock. While he's making love to my pussy I suck the tip of his cock into my mouth, tasting his semen. He groans and the sound buzzes against my inner lips. I can't wait.

I turn and impale myself on his hard shaft, using my thigh muscles to lift and lower my body on his staff. I reach down and rub my clit, both in my dream and in reality, until I come, juices running freely.

I said at the beginning of this story that my fantasy flashed before my eyes. When? Why? Well, I met Chad at a local club and now he's here with me, naked, his arms stretched above his head, waiting willingly for me to fasten his wrists to the headboard of my bed. He's not the stud I fantasized about, but he's here, ready, hard.

I heave a long, low sigh of pleasure.

# We'll Never Get This Done

"WOULD YOU EVER CONSIDER DOING SOMETHING LIKE that?" Keith asked as he and his wife, Emily, watched an erotic video in their bedroom.

"Do what?" Emily said. "We have oral sex all the time."

"I mean shave your bush like that woman does."

Emily had been paying only mild attention to the film. She wasn't much into videos but she loved that they put her husband of three years in the mood. Their sex life was fabulous and they did wonderfully creative things in bed but she secretly feared that over the long haul things might get stale. She always looked for new stuff for the bedroom but this film was a little dull so she'd tuned out.

When she focused her attention on the screen she saw a close-up crotch shot of a woman with her pubic area totally bare. Well, not totally, she realized. She'd left a tiny heart-shaped area on her pubic bone unshaved. "I really never thought about it."

"It must make oral sex a whole new thing. I mean, I can see so much more on her," he said, indicating the siliconed woman on the screen. "She's not much to look at, pretty phony and all, but seeing her pussy like that, almost totally naked . . ."

Emily turned and snuggled against her husband, resting a hand against the crotch of his jeans. He was rock hard. "Really turns you on, doesn't it?" She loved it that they could talk so openly about sex.

"Yeah," he said sheepishly. "I mean, I wouldn't want you to do anything that might hurt or anything." He didn't take his eyes off the screen. In the film the guy was fingering the woman's naked snatch and flicking his tongue over her clit. "Would you think about it? It's so hot."

"I guess my only worry would be about the itchiness when it grows in," Emily added. "My sister told me that, after her kids were born, the growing-in process was a bitch."

"Listen, if it's going to be trouble afterward, it wouldn't be worth it." He watched with rapt attention for a few moments until the scene shifted to straight fucking. "Maybe those women do something to soften the hair up so it doesn't scratch."

"Makes you really hot, doesn't it," Emily said. It wasn't a question.

"I'll show you how much," he said, rolling on top of her and kissing her soundly. As the DVD played on, the two pulled off their clothes and made quick, hot love.

The following day Emily thought a lot about what Keith had suggested. If it appealed to Keith, despite the obvious downside, she'd do a little serious research. She surfed the Internet and found several sites that discussed shaving and ways to keep the area from getting irritated. They recommended lots of different remedies: aftershave, alcohol, drying the area thoroughly, using an antibiotic ointment afterward and lots of expensive creams and lotions. She read everything and finally decided that, with a few precautions, it might be worth a try.

The following weekend she brought it up with Keith. After dinner and a little wine to bolster her courage, she said, "Would you like to try your hand at shaving my pussy?" She watched his eyes light up. "Maybe I could look like those girls in the movies."

"I would love that," he said, suddenly alert, "but you told me about all the problems. I didn't think you'd be interested."

"I did some research on the net and got a few ideas to try to minimize the aftereffects. I distilled them down to the ones that occurred most often. Want to give it a shot?"

"Holy shit, babe, I'd love to, but why have me do it? Shouldn't you do it yourself so you can take care not to cut yourself and all?"

"Many of the sites suggest that someone else do the job. You can see what you're doing, and I know you'll be careful."

He hesitated. "Are you sure you trust me not to nick your beautiful skin?" He looked genuinely concerned.

"If you don't want to . . ."

"Hon, you know I do. It's just a little scary. I wouldn't want to hurt you in any way."

"I know that, silly, but it's erotic as hell and I love what it does to both of us. Let's give it a try."

"If you're sure."

"I'm sure. Let me take a hot shower and gather a few of the things we'll need."

Emily took a quick shower and washed her bush carefully and thoroughly. Then, wrapped in a towel, she wandered into the bedroom holding a pair of scissors. "I'm ready for phase one." She snicked the scissors. "We've got to trim the hairs really short. It will help you to see what you're doing later."

She stretched out crosswise on the bed, feet on the floor, and arranged the towel beneath her buttocks. Her nipples were erect and she knew she was wet from more than the shower, but also at the prospect of Keith's ministrations.

He crouched between her knees and stared at his wife's body. "We're really going to do this, aren't we?"

Emily could only grin at the leer on her husband's face and the heat in his gaze. "Oh yeah, love. We certainly are."

Slowly and with great care Keith trimmed his wife's bush. Then he gathered up the towel with the clippings and put it aside. His tongue quickly found his wife's clit, now easily seen through the shortened hair. Emily heard her own raspy breathing and her heart pounded. Keith knew just where to lick. He lightly sucked her inner lips into his mouth, then made a slight humming sound. The buzzing between her legs was irresistible and when his fingers slid inside her sopping passage she shook with the force of her climax.

Keith was quickly naked and his hard cock found her easily. Only a few strokes and she felt him convulse. Later she said, "At this rate, we'll never really do this."

"Maybe tomorrow night," Keith mumbled sleepily.

"Maybe," she said, pulling the covers over them both.

The following evening they had a pizza delivered and both wolfed down slices. "Ready for the next phase?" Keith said.

"If it turns out like last evening, I'm more than ready." She took another shower and again settled on the bed. "This will require a little self-control. Most of the sites I visited on the Web suggest that we dry the area thoroughly and keep it dry for a while afterward. I think that means keeping me dry."

"Difficult to do when you get so wet so easily," Keith said with a wide grin. "No self-restraint at all." He slowly shook his head.

"You're the problem," Emily said with a laugh.

"Okay. We'll both try to be good."

"Right. Anyway, here's a new disposable razor and some shaving foam with antibiotics. Don't get the soap inside me, but otherwise go for it."

Looking very serious, Keith again knelt between his wife's thighs and began to apply foam to her mound. "That feel okay?" he asked.

"It feels fabulous." She felt her body moistening from the feel of Keith's fingers touching her both intimately and clinically.

"Remember self-control," he said.

"I can't help what my body does," she said with a shiver.

Keith continued to shave her mound. "They say that you should not go over the area too much. One or two strokes with the razor should do it. You can always do more tomorrow."

When her mound was clean shaven, he said, "I'm afraid to do the insides of your thighs and your inner lips. It's all so close to your pussy."

"It's all right," she said trying not to tremble. "Go for it."

As he slowly stroked the blade over her thighs and outer lips, she knew she'd had enough. "Put the razor down," she said, "and fuck me right now."

"But I haven't finished the job," he said with a chuckle.

"To hell with finishing the job. Finish me instead."

He finished her with his mouth and his fingers, then climbed onto the bed and held her head to his cock while she licked and sucked. Again it took only moments for him to fill her mouth with his semen.

Later he got a wet cloth and a towel from the bathroom and carefully washed then dried his wife's newly shaven mound.

"We didn't complete the job," Keith said. "I still have to shave the area around your opening and toward the back too."

"Who the hell cares?" Emily said. "I hope we never get done."

Once Emily was in position the next night, Keith couldn't resist the urge to get one of their favorite toys, a long, thick dildo, and watch as it slid in and out of his wife's mostly shaved body. "God, this is so fabulous," he said as he fucked his wife with the toy. "I can see your clit swell and watch your juice trickle between your ass cheeks." Emily was surprised that, in addition to his play, his words pushed her over the edge.

The following evening Keith got ready to continue the job, but merely looking at his wife's mostly shaved groin was enough to end their shaving session and begin an hour of passion, this time with an anal dildo.

They will get it done. Eventually.

## *Porn Star*

❧

$\mathcal{O}$NE SATURDAY MORNING OVER COFFEE, SANDY'S HUSBAND, Dan, suggested that they buy a video camera. "They've really come down in price," he said. "There's an ad here in the paper for one for less than two hundred dollars." He read from the ad. "It records for sixty minutes and has five-point-six megapixels, whatever they are."

"Hon, you don't know enough about them to know whether we're buying the right one and not spending too much."

"We can ask the guys in the store. They'll know everything."

Dan and Sandy spent almost an hour with the salesman in the electronics superstore, looking over cameras and camcorders, learning about megapixels, flash cards and things Sandy wasn't sure she understood even after the guy explained them. Sandy wandered off to look over some DVDs, so the salesman talked to Dan. "Okay, let's say you want to take pictures of your kids."

"No kids."

"Man, you're lucky. I got four so my wife and I get no privacy anymore."

What was the purpose of that segue? Dan wondered. In response to his raised eyebrow, the man said, "For taking movies. You know." He glanced over at Sandy, attractive in a pair of tight-fitting jeans and a striped blouse.

Still puzzled, Dan said, "Sorry?"

"I didn't mean to say anything. Forget it."

"Forget what?"

"Movies. You and your wife. Lots of folks who come in to buy a camera intend to take sexy videos." He cleared his throat. "Sorry if I offended you."

A small smile crept over Dan's face. He'd had the idea in the back of his mind but he figured it might be a little too "out there" for Sandy. However, if it was ordinary enough for this guy to be talking about it . . .

"If you ever decide to get into that," the salesman said, "there are a few Web sites that have great tips for taking erotic movies."

"I don't think so," Dan said, tempted to take the information but sure that his wife wouldn't be interested.

When Sandy returned to where the two men were standing, they talked for a few more minutes. "Whatever you want, hon," she said.

Dan took that as an omen that maybe his dreams might eventually come true, so he finally settled on a camera, a case, extra memory cards and a few other accessories, spending almost three hundred dollars.

At home later, they read all the directions, charged the battery and then experimented taking pictures of each other. They learned quickly about lighting and distances, then went outside and took movies around the neighborhood.

It was like magic. Point, press the button and watch the movies on screen on the back of the camera. Then they downloaded the clips to their computer and watched again. Late that afternoon, Dan said, "The guy at the store mentioned that we could get connectors so we could watch the films on the big TV. I think I'll run over there and pick them up."

"Good idea," Sandy said. "That will make it much easier to watch what we film even in the bedroom. And I think the guy said that if we film in the house, we can watch live, as we're taking the pictures. Listen, honey, I've got a few things to do around here so you go ahead." As he opened the front door Sandy called, "Don't spend too much."

Film? In the house? In the bedroom? Was she suggesting something?

Back at the electronics store, he found the salesman, waited until he finished with his customer, then asked, "You said you knew of Web sites with information about taking erotic videos."

The man beamed, wrote something on a slip of paper and handed it to Dan. "That site will fix you up real good." He also got the connectors Dan needed to hook the camera to the TV.

That evening he booted up the computer. The site the guy had suggested did, indeed, have tips, but more important, it had suggestions about how to entice a partner into making erotic movies. He read most, then found something that he thought would appeal. A few more mouse clicks and he was ready.

"Hey, hon," he called, "I want to show you something."

Sandy, book in hand, wandered into the den. On the screen was a woman in a sexy peignoir, carefully made up, hair perfectly combed. The caption read, "Glamour Pix."

"This company does a complete makeover, gets you all dolled up, then takes photos." He sighed. "I'd love to see you do that."

"Not a chance," Sandy said. "It's all so phony."

"I'd love to have a picture of you like that, though."

"Well, you'd have to take it yourself. No way am I going to parade around in front of some total stranger."

"Would you let me do that?" Dan said, having fully expected Sandy's reaction.

"Are you serious?"

"Sure. You could do your hair and makeup, then wear that thing your sister got you last Christmas."

"Nah," she said, "I'd feel like a tart." She might believe it was wrong, but her eyes seemed to say something different, something erotic.

Dan pulled her down onto his lap. "What's wrong with that? It would just be between us and I'd really like it. Maybe a movie of you looking really fabulous."

"No one else would ever see it, right?"

"Of course not."

"It might be fun, I guess."

"How about tomorrow evening?"

\*   \*   \*

THE FOLLOWING MORNING THE COUPLE PLAYED TENNIS
with some friends; then Dan mowed the lawn while Sandy put-
tered around the house. Dan couldn't help but dream that she
was bathing, washing her hair and doing all sorts of delicious
things to get herself ready for the movie shoot, as he was start-
ing to think of it.

They had take-out Chinese for dinner; then, with a con-
spiratorial wink, Sandy disappeared. Trying not to think about
what she might be doing, he logged on to the computer and
surfed a few sites devoted to making erotic films and one that
specialized in amateur videos. An hour later, she called, "Dan,
come into the bedroom."

As he walked down the hall he hoped, prayed, dreamed. He
was rewarded. Sandy lay in an erotic pose on the bed, wearing
the black satin and lace gown she'd gotten from her sister. She
had added long, black net stockings and black high-heeled pumps.
Her hair was fluffed out and she had used lots of eye makeup and
lipstick. She looked like a porn star. He gasped.

"Like it?"

"Like it? You're fabulous. I never saw you looking any sex-
ier." He rubbed his hand over the tent at the front of his jeans.
"Shit, baby, you're hot!"

Her smile showed her white teeth. "Want to take my picture?"

"Sure." He got the camera and took a few moments of video
of her on the bed. "It's a bit dull if you don't move around.
Why don't you tease me a little while I hold the camera?"

She turned onto her hands and knees and crawled toward him, giving him and the camera a great view of her breasts down the front of her gown. Then she blew kisses at him, which the camera caught easily.

"This is recording sound too, you know," Dan said.

"Right. Well, baby, this is for you, and you alone. I'm here, waiting for you."

"Are you hot for me?"

"I'm sopping wet just thinking about it."

"Show me."

"How?" Sandy said, looking puzzled.

"Play with your tits or something."

Taking his advice, Sandy lifted her breasts, then teased her satin-covered nipples, something Dan knew made her really hungry.

"Let the top down so I can see."

Sandy hesitated, then slipped the straps of the gown from her shoulders, playing peekaboo with her breasts. At one point the lace of the gown caught on one erect nipple, hanging for a moment, driving Dan crazy. "Oh," Sandy said with mock innocence, "sorry."

"Don't be sorry. It's sexy as hell."

Sandy grinned. "I hoped it would be."

Then the gown was bunched down at her waist and she was squeezing and stroking handfuls of her breast flesh, then offering it for him to taste. He wanted to indulge but he hoped for more from this movie.

"Okay, how about taking off the gown completely so I can see everything."

Sandy was a sexy woman, but very private. He was surprised that she seemed to have completely forgotten the camera he was holding. She wiggled out of the gown and tossed it away, then settled back onto the bed. "Like this?" she said, her breathing husky.

"Baby, you're fabulous." He hesitated. He might ruin it all, but he had to try. "Can I have a look at your bush?"

She twisted onto her knees, then ran her fingers through her pubic hair. "It's here for you."

"Damn, baby, you're driving me nuts."

"So put that thing down and join me."

Dan turned the camera off, put it on the dresser and quickly stripped off his clothes and piled them on a chair. Then he climbed onto the bed beside her as Sandy parted her legs to give him a good look at her swollen tissues. "God, I'm so wet," she said, running her fingertips over her inner lips.

Then, hands wet, she grasped his hard cock in slippery fingers and slid her hands up and down his shaft. "It seems that I'm not the only one who's excited around here."

"Shit, baby, keep doing that and I'll waste it in your hand."

"No waste," she said, continuing to manipulate Dan's erection. It took only a moment until he was ready to come. He tried to push onto Sandy's body but she held him, continuing to fondle his cock. Then she brought her mouth near it, licking her lips in an exaggerated pantomime of sucking him. He couldn't hold back any longer. Eyes closed, spurts of semen jetted from his cock.

A few moments later he felt Sandy move beside him and he opened his eyes. "Damn, baby, that was amazing."

She pouted. "It was, of course, but you left me hanging." She took his hand and put it on her pussy. "Fix it."

He loved masturbating her and he quickly found her clit and softly stroked it, listening to her little moans of pleasure. She reached out and grabbed a dildo from her bedside table. "Use this," she panted.

Nonplussed but eager, he took the slender shaft and slid it into her, then fucked her until she was screaming with ecstasy. "Yes, yes, yes," she screamed. "Do it. Don't stop. Like that. Like that."

With a yell, she came, then became totally limp.

It was several minutes before either of them was coherent enough to speak. "Holy shit, baby," Dan said. "That was amazing."

Sandy's grin covered her entire face. "Yeah, it was. And I think the camera got most of it."

Startled, Dan had thought she'd forgotten the video. "Camera? I turned it off."

"I turned it back on while you were undressing."

"You're kidding." He got up and looked at the camera. It was indeed running, and pointed directly at the bed. He flipped it off.

"Not at all. I was wondering how long it would take you to realize what fun we could have with it."

"You mean . . . ?"

"You're not the only one with a deliciously dirty mind. Just imagine what fun we can have watching the video over and over on the big screen."

"Damn, I knew I married you for a reason."

# *Subways Aren't for Sleeping*

⚜

*B*EFORE I BEGIN MY TALE, LET ME TELL YOU JUST A TINY bit about myself. I'm a reasonably attractive woman of thirty-four. I've got short, curly brown hair, brown eyes, but none of that matters really because the guys in my dreams don't ever look at my face.

I don't wear panties anymore. I live in New York City, and last summer was a really hot one. Much of the city is air-conditioned as are the subways now. But the platforms are a disaster and with all the people waiting for trains it quickly becomes oppressive. So last summer I stopped wearing sticky, icky undies. And I love to wear skirts. When the train arrives there's a blast of air ahead of the front car that whistles up my legs and cools my pussy, a part that constantly needs cooling.

I don't start my secretarial job until ten, so it was just after rush hour one morning. The train pulled into the station and the cooling breezes caressed my labia. I was cool, but hot at the same time. The air reminded me of how long it had been since I had a good fucking. My mind wandered and I was only barely aware of getting on the train and finding a seat. Since I go against the usual traffic, I often get to sit. Anyway, I became aware of the guy sitting directly opposite me.

I don't know whether the breeze had revealed my bare thighs, or flattened my skirt against my butt but from his expression I thought he suspected that I was naked beneath. For whatever reason he was gazing longingly at my legs. I crossed them, then recrossed them the other way. His eyes moved to my face and he smiled at me.

He was wearing a dark blue business suit and carrying a briefcase. He wasn't really good-looking, but his smile was attractive and sort of inviting. And it went all the way to his blue eyes. I smiled back, but in the New York subway you have to be really careful, so I looked away.

Several minutes later I glanced back at him and he was still smiling at me, sort of quiet and shy. Then his gaze went from my face to my crotch. He did know. I again uncrossed and recrossed my legs, feeling a slight wetness between my thighs that had nothing to do with the heat of the day. I slid the palm of my hand into the small of my back, lifted my butt just a bit and smoothed the fabric over my ass. To do this, I had to uncross my legs again.

He stared and his smile widened just a bit.

*Okay*, I told myself. *Let's see what happens.*

I didn't recross my legs. Rather, I let my knees part just a bit. He licked his lips.

The train slowed and stopped. People walked between us to get to the car doors, exited, and more people piled on. There were enough empty seats to go around so, as the train left the station the guy and I were again able to see each other. I thought about what he must be seeing, a woman with her knees slightly parted, and, to the best of his knowledge, nothing between his gaze and her bush but her lightweight, full skirt. He raised his eyebrow slightly, as if daring me.

Do I take dares?

You bet. I parted my knees a little more. The shadow between my thighs must have been getting deeper. He licked his lips again and I got wetter. And wetter. I had the picture of him getting up, settling next to me and putting his hand between my legs. He didn't, of course, but the mental image caused my clit to swell.

His gaze was hot and again his eyebrow lifted.

I glanced around and, to my surprise, no one else seemed aware of our little drama. I would have thought the heat of both his stare and my crotch would have alerted everyone, but the rest of the occupants of the car continued to read or listen to their iPods, totally oblivious.

*Okay,* I told myself, *no one else is watching. What harm can there be?* I spread my knees wide so he could get a good view of my snatch. For good measure I adjusted my skirt so it rode high on my thighs, enhancing the scene.

He grinned, moved his briefcase from his lap to the floor between his shoes, then placed his hand on his crotch, outlining a fine-looking erection.

I pressed my knees together and rubbed my thighs against

each other, wondering whether I'd have a giant wet spot on the back of my skirt. Who the hell cared? I moved so my sopping lips squished against each other, and the guy rubbed his cock.

The train stopped again and more riders moved between us.

When the area between us was clear again we continued our play, me rubbing my thighs, then spreading my knees, him not too subtly stroking his erection. I almost came. Right there on the number four train.

As the subway slowed for another stop, the guy looked up, seemed startled, then leaped from his seat as the door opened. He rushed through the sliding doors, then stopped outside the window where he could see me. He quickly unzipped, pulled out an enormous cock, rubbed it and, just as quickly, zipped it back into his pants.

I went to the ladies' room when I got to my office and, totally frustrated, slipped into a stall and rubbed my clit until I came with a tiny gasp of pleasure. When I had dried myself thoroughly I looked at my back in the mirror and was happy to see no wet spot on my skirt. I pictured the guy dashing into the men's room and jerking off until his cock spurted into the toilet.

God, I loved that thought.

I haven't found another guy quite so responsive but I keep riding the same train, hoping to see him again. I wonder whether I'd have the nerve this time to move beside him and caress his erection myself. I wonder . . .

Dear Reader,

I know you've enjoyed my stories and I hope they give you the hunger to read more. I've written several other collections: *Bedtime Stories for Lovers, Naughty Bedtime Stories, Naughtier Bedtime Stories* and *Bawdy Bedtime Stories.* They all contain many more fun tales to spice up your evenings.

I'd love it if you'd drop me a note and let me know which of these stories proved to be your particular favorites. That way I'll know what to write more of when I put together another collection. Drop me a note at JoanELloyd@att.net. And please visit my website, www.joanelloyd.com. You can read about all my books, novels, nonfiction and short stories. Also, please check out the forums for letters and information on dozens of sexual topics.

—Joan

Printed in the United States
by Baker & Taylor Publisher Services